The Poker Face of Murder

A ROSE CRUZ COZY MURDER MYSTERY BOOK 4

Audrey Alden

Copyright © **2025 by Audrey Alden**

All rights reserved.

No part of this publication may be reproduced, distributed, or transmitted in any form or by any means, including photocopying, recording, or other electronic or mechanical methods, without the prior written permission of the publisher, except as permitted by U.S. copyright law. For permission requests, contact info@audreyaldenauthor.com.

The story, all names, characters, and incidents portrayed in this production are fictitious. No identification with actual persons (living or deceased), places, buildings, and products is intended or should be inferred.

Contents

Introduction	V
Prologue	1
Chapter 1	7
Chapter 2	14
Chapter 3	22
Chapter 4	29
Chapter 5	35
Chapter 6	43
Chapter 7	49
Chapter 8	55
Chapter 9	62
Chapter 10	69
Chapter 11	75
Chapter 12	83
Chapter 13	89

Chapter 14	95
Chapter 15	103
Chapter 16	109
Chapter 17	115
Chapter 18	122
Chapter 19	129
Chapter 20	136
Chapter 21	142
Chapter 22	148
Chapter 23	157
Chapter 24	164
Chapter 25	170
Chapter 26	177
Chapter 27	184
Chapter 28	190
Chapter 29	197
Epilogue	204
Sneak Peek	209

Introduction

The Midnight Tide's poker tournament should be all glitz, glamour, and high stakes—until a deadly hand is dealt.

When a notorious high-roller is found lifeless in his suite, his winnings vanished and two golden poker chips eerily placed over his eyes, Cruise Director Rose Dela Cruz knows this isn't just a simple robbery gone wrong.

As whispers swirl through the ship's elegant halls, Rose and her loyal beagle Rex follow a trail of counterfeit chips, tampered casino footage, and buried grudges that run deeper than anyone suspects.

With the clock ticking toward the ship's next port, every friendly smile hides a secret, and every ally could be the one holding the winning card — or the deadly ace.

In a game where trust is the ultimate gamble, Rose must uncover the truth before the killer disappears beneath the waves... and justice is lost to the sea.

Prologue
The Night Luck Ran Out

Something's not right.

The sharp beep of the phone call disconnecting rings in my ear, making my heart skip a beat. What could one of the guests possibly mean by a commotion on the upper decks?

My mind immediately jumps to the worst-case scenario: ribbons of red staining a luxurious suite's carpet, intricate bloody patterns soaking into the fibers, spreading like wildfire.

Rex's soft whimper pulls me back from the spiral of dark thoughts, grounding me in the present.

I glance down at him, forcing a smile I know is more for me than for him. "I'm sure it's nothing, right, bud?"

Rex sits up, his hind legs firm on the floor, licking his nose like he hasn't a care in the world. His calm is a balm to my nerves—even if it doesn't fully ease the knot twisting in my stomach. My Rex—a super dog, if I say so myself—doesn't sniff out blood or danger.

So it must be fine.

It has to be fine.

I shake my head, pushing the dark thoughts away. I've had enough tragedies to last a lifetime. As my therapist always says, most things are out of my control.

But here I am, still standing. The Midnight Tide charts a new course—from Miami to San Juan—and I'm slowly learning the rhythm of the casino.

After all, this is the first time we're holding a poker tournament onboard.

That reminds me—I still need to follow up on Jasper Thorne and his suspiciously fast winnings. Everyone at the table said the same thing: Who can win that much money that quickly? It's... curious, to say the least.

See?

I've got too much on my plate already. And now, a commotion?

Focus, Rose, I tell myself, planting my feet firmly on the deck.

The ship shudders beneath my soles, the deep vibrations of The Midnight Tide anchoring me in the moment. If I ignore it, maybe it'll just go away.

I take a steadying breath and move forward, step by step. Rex follows close behind, tail wagging as if he knows exactly where we're headed.

Maybe he does—I wouldn't put it past him.

I pass the ship's casino—the one place I avoid when I can. It hums with frenetic energy, a swirl of excitement and anxiety mixed with the clatter of coins, whirring wheels, and shuffling cards.

It's almost overwhelming, yet oddly comforting—like the heartbeat of the ship itself.

But I'm moving away from it now—away from the buzz and chaos—toward something unknown.

I walk past the promenade deck, the Sunset Bar, the souvenir shop, the main hall, and the sounds fade behind me. Up a few flights of stairs, I find myself on the upper deck, near the presidential suites.

The old woman who called earlier stands in the hallway. Her cardigan is pulled tight around her shoulders, hands trembling as she spots me in my sharp suit and glinting name tag.

She hurries over, voice shaking. "You're the cruise director, right? The one I called?"

"Yeah, that's me..." My throat tightens, something heavy pressing down on my chest.

I can feel it deep in my bones.

Something is very wrong.

"It's the room next door," she whispers urgently, glancing over her shoulder like she expects someone to appear. "I heard... thumping, things falling. Like two people wrestling on the floor."

I look toward the door she points at. A chill runs up my spine, prickling my skin. The hairs on the back of my neck rise.

It's Jasper Thorne's room.

"I'll check it out. Thanks for calling me," I say with a smile that I hope comforts her. It doesn't comfort me. My nerves tighten as I take one step after another toward Jasper's suite.

Suddenly, my senses sharpen.

The ship's vibrations feel stronger beneath my feet, louder in my ears. I hear the ocean slicing against the metal hull. The old lady's mutters sound like whispers right beside me. The faint hum and crackle of electricity overhead become distinct. Even the lights above seem brighter when I glance up.

I'm reeling—no, stop.

I suck in a deep breath, ribs expanding under my skin. Then I exhale slowly.

I'm okay; I have to be. The last thing I need is to let anxiety take over.

With Rex nudging my leg, I find comfort in knowing I'm not alone. With newfound confidence and my loyal companion, I finally reach Jasper's suite. The white door and gold lettering above the peephole are familiar.

I lift my finger and press the doorbell.

Thirteen... fourteen... fifteen seconds pass, nothing.

I knock. "Mr. Thorne? Are you in there?"

Silence.

Moments like this make my skin prickle—the silence, the stillness, and the dread that follows.

So I pull out the master keycard Ben gave me, tap it against the door sensor. As soon as it glows green, I twist the knob and step inside. I don't second-guess whether Jasper is asleep or in the bathroom—my gut knows something's wrong.

As I enter, Rex lets out a low, almost inaudible whimper. The room smells less like our usual citrus and white tea, more like sweat.

The presidential suites follow the same layout: a living space leading to a balcony, a door to the right opening into the bedroom, and beyond that, the bathroom.

The living room is empty. Nothing disturbed. No blood on the carpet.

But it's too soon to feel relieved.

"Mr. Thorne? Are you here?" I call into the quiet.

No answer.

Rex charges ahead, whatever fear he had is gone. He tugs on his leash, pulling me toward the bedroom.

I let Rex lead me; between the two of us, he's always been the insightful one.

A few steps later, I'm standing in the bedroom doorway. Whatever calm filled the living room, it's the exact opposite here—pure havoc.

The bedside table has toppled over, and the lamp that usually sits on it lies shattered on the floor. A cup of water spilled and broke, shards of glass scattered across the carpet—I instinctively pull Rex back to keep him safe. The duvet is half-sliding off the bed, and the pillows are thrown in every direction.

But that's not the worst part.

The worst part is Jasper—sprawled in the middle of the room, motionless... maybe even limp. Too limp for someone alive.

"Mr. Thorne!" I rush to his side and kneel, but his face makes me recoil a few inches.

I've seen my share of horrors before, but this is different. There's no blood, no weapon. Instead, two gold poker chips are deliberately placed over his eyes.

It's... peculiar.

Shaking off the shock, I crawl back and press two fingers against the side of his neck, searching for a pulse. Hoping to find the faint beat that means life.

But nothing.

My breath hitches, then shudders. My lungs deflate while my chest tightens, as if invisible icy fingers are squeezing my throat, trying to suffocate me.

I can't breathe.

I can't move.

I can't think.

Only for a moment.

That fleeting moment stretches into an eternity—paralyzing terror crawling beneath my skin and rattling my bones.

But I won't let it take me.

I force a shaky inhale and exhale, grounding myself in this brutal reality.

The shock swells and recedes in seconds, and then my eyes dart frantically around the room, searching for the killer—just in case.

Every shadow stretches into a threat. Every inanimate object seems alive, ready to strike. Every corner, doorway, piece of furniture hides some phantom of Jasper's murderer.

Mustering what courage I have, I stand on trembling legs and open the bathroom door. It's empty.

I scan the bedroom again and spot Rex sniffing something in the corner—two one-hundred-dollar bills, oddly out of place, like they've been tossed or dropped.

It hits me—Jasper's suspicious winnings from earlier.

Right... could this be a robbery gone wrong?

I start searching for Jasper's black bag, the one he carried from the casino with his winnings—hundreds of thousands of dollars. I'm careful not to disturb anything, wanting to preserve the crime scene, but it's nowhere to be found.

Could someone really have come in to steal it?

Maybe.

But look at Jasper.

A voice in my head pushes me to study the scene: a dead man with two gold poker chips over his eyes.

No robber would stage a scene like this.

This attack was deliberate—planned and executed to kill.

And those gold poker chips...

They're a message.

But what does it mean?

Chapter 1
Five Days Before the Incident

"Miami, Florida... ahh." Stacy Dela Cruz, my sister, takes a deep, dramatic breath the moment we step onto the cement docks of the Port of Miami. She wrinkles her nose and adds, "It smells like salt air and... diesel."

"Well, it's a dock, sweetheart." Cole Hester, her boyfriend, smiles as he gently brushes the small of her back. He's also my coworker—the head of security on The Midnight Tide.

Just a few weeks ago, these two would've been too embarrassed to show any affection in front of us, having kept their relationship secret for months. But now? Look at them. Honestly, a sight for sore eyes.

I can't help but laugh, shaking my head in mild amusement.

"Oh my gosh, I'm really here!" Behind me, Julia Hart—the ever-energetic assistant who never knows when to stop bouncing—squeals while hopping up and down in her bright yellow sundress, complete with a giant bow on her matching sun hat.

Julia's known for her eccentric style, but with all the colors around us, who can blame her for wanting to stand out?

At her feet, Rex, my beagle, wags his tail like crazy, almost like he understands what this trip means for Julia.

It's her first time outside Europe, thanks to The Midnight Tide's newest route, which begins right here in Miami. So here we are.

"Okay, calm down, Julia," I say with a smile, feeling her infectious excitement ripple up my arms and paint warmth across my cheeks. It makes my grin grow even wider. "There's still more to be excited about, you know?"

"Oh, I can tell!" Julia beams, eyes wide as she takes in the dock's buzz.

The city's energy hits like a warm tropical hug, like being wrapped inside a coconut lined with tiny paper umbrellas. A kaleidoscope of pastel Art Deco buildings dances above us while the sparkling cerulean waters of Biscayne Bay stretch behind.

Floating on those waters is The Midnight Tide—sleek hull, modern design, panoramic views, balconies lining every deck, and a promenade circling the ship like a silver ribbon.

Just below the gangway, Ben Anderson, our captain, bids farewell to the last of the crew. Then he turns, heading toward us.

Under the blazing sun, his dark hair shines, and those blue eyes look sharper than ever. When our gazes lock, his lips curl into that easy smile I've come to know all too well. Sometimes I wonder how I got so lucky to be dating him.

"Sorry to keep you all waiting," Ben says, squinting against the glare overhead. "The company just confirmed all our accommodations are ready. There's a guy waiting for us at the parking lot to take us to our new home."

"New home?" Stacy echoes, eyes sparkling. "Please tell me I'm part of that—as an . . . honorary employee of The Midnight Tide."

Ben chuckles and casually takes my hand as we start toward the parking lot. "I made sure they know you'll be staying with Rose . . . or Cole, whichever you prefer."

I snicker. We aren't kids embarrassed about living with our partners anymore, but it's still kind of funny watching my usually confident older sister blush.

"Shut up, Rose," Stacy shoots back, rolling her eyes. "You realize I can annoy you twice as much once we're at our new place, right? Just so you know, I'm sticking to you until you get tired of me."

"Only if Cole agrees." I glance at Cole, who smiles shyly.

"She can stay wherever she wants. She's the boss," Cole says with a grin.

We laugh.

Just like that, the five of us—six, including Rex—walk from the dock to the parking lot, where a van waits to take us to Ocean Drive and our new apartment, courtesy of The Midnight Tide.

It's only about twenty minutes, thanks to company cars provided while we're in the city. Perks of working for the cruise line.

Soon, the driver drops us off in front of a white apartment building. Simple, modern, sleek lines with minimalistic design. Wrought-iron balconies decorate every floor of the six-story building.

Palm trees frame the scene, swaying gently in the ocean breeze. Because it wouldn't be Miami without palms, right?

We all step out and thank the driver. Ben pulls out keys to our rooms—all on the sixth floor: 6-A for Stacy and me, 6-B for Ben, 6-C for Cole, and 6-D for Julia.

"Wait..." Julia says, taking her key, a resin keychain with sand and a tiny shell trapped inside it. "Does this mean we're all staying in the same building?"

Before Ben can answer, Julia's already squealing and spinning in place. "Oh, what a dream! I get to live on the same floor as all of you!"

We exchange amused glances and chuckle.

Without delay, we escape the ninety-degree heat and head up to the sixth floor.

The apartment takes my breath away. Sunlight floods the open layout through huge windows. White walls, hardwood floors, and the living, dining, and kitchen spaces flow seamlessly into one another.

The living room has a leather L-shaped couch, a coffee table, and an abstract painting on the wall. The dining area holds a glass table that seats six, surrounded by white chairs. The kitchen boasts white cabinets and a roomy island.

In the center of the living room, luggage and boxes wait for Stacy and me—our things had been delivered ahead for a smooth move-in.

While the others settle into their apartments, Stacy races to her bedroom. It has floor-to-ceiling windows and a queen-sized bed. Even Rex darts around, already settling into our temporary home.

"This is amazing!" Stacy spins, fingers grazing every surface. She heads to the kitchen, opening cupboards to find them empty. "Well, first on the list—groceries."

"Already noted," I say, dropping onto the couch, letting the cool leather soothe my sweaty back.

Stacy jumps next to me, stretching out on the other side of the couch. "Oh, and we have to try sushi! I read we can roller-skate on the beach and, at night, dance to some Latin music. What do you think?"

When it comes to being the life of the party, leave it to Stacy to have a fun-filled—but somewhat exhausting—itinerary. Still, I chuckle. "That'd be great if my bedtime wasn't 10:00 p.m."

"Boo!" Stacy shoots me a thumbs-down. "We just got to a new city. You have to live a little, you know? If you ask me, the real cure for your nightmares is pina coladas."

Even with Stacy's teasing wink, I feel only a slight relief.

She's right—I do need to 'cure' these nightmares. But pina coladas? I doubt they'll do the trick. Instead, Ben and I have already found a therapist in town who specializes in trauma recovery—though I'm not exactly ready to call what I'm dealing with trauma.

Maybe that's just me, still in denial.

I sit up straighter and tell Stacy, "Actually, Ben and I will be off this afternoon. We found this new therapist, and I'll be seeing her."

"Really?" Stacy sits up too, reaching out to squeeze my knee. "That's great, Rose! I'm sure it'll do wonders."

"I hope so, too." I offer her a weak smile. "But before that, I thought I saw some food trucks right across the street. Want to check them out?"

Stacy jumps up and fixes her hair. "I could use some tacos. Let's go!"

Right then, Stacy, Rex, and I leave the apartment, ready for some much-needed sisterly time.

We cross the street to the food trucks, grabbing fruit shakes, tacos, and even snow cones. Rex makes the rounds, greeting strangers, and even scores his own little hot dog in a bun.

Afterward, we stop at a convenience store to pick up some essentials for the apartment. The farmer's market can wait—we still have time.

When we get back, Ben is already waiting just outside the hallway.

"I'll just get changed," I tell him, "then we can go."

In ten minutes, I'm back out, walking hand in hand with Ben toward the parking lot.

We climb into Ben's new company-issued car—a white SUV. He leans over to help buckle my seatbelt, and I laugh at how unnecessary it is. "You know I can do this myself, right?"

Ben chuckles, face close to mine before pulling away and clicking on his own belt. "I know you can, but can you just let me do the little things?"

"Fine." I fake a groan, though something flutters in my chest every time Ben is sweet.

Once we're on the road, I reach over and take his hand, resting it on the armrest. Our fingers intertwine.

"Thanks for coming with me, Ben."

He squeezes my hand. "I promise I'll come with you to all your sessions from now on, Rose."

At first, I was ashamed of my nightmares. But Ben convinced me it's okay to be vulnerable. So with him, I am.

He's been opening up more too. Despite all these months together, I feel like I'm seeing a new side of him—someone more sincere. Someone with depth worth diving into.

I hope Ben sees that same side of me.

When we arrive at the therapist's office, Ben waits in the lobby while I meet Dr. Lorraine West.

She's a beautiful woman, with long brown hair falling almost to her waist, and a soft smile that makes me feel warm and fuzzy inside.

"Hi, Rose. I'm so glad to finally meet you." Lorraine's eyes are curious and friendly—not intimidating like some of the therapists I've seen before.

I sit on the couch across from her and smile back. "Thanks for having me, Dr. West."

"Oh, please, Lorraine will do," she says.

I nod. "If you insist, Lorraine."

Her smile grows bigger. "There you go. Now, let's get started, shall we? Tell me, Rose: What brought you here today?"

I've sat in similar chairs with similar people over the past few months, but I still get nervous explaining to strangers why I need their help.

Still, knowing Stacy and Ben want me to take this seriously, I lean back into the couch and say, "I've been having nightmares about the . . . bad things I've seen back on the cruise ship I work on. And I'm always kind of on my toes, waiting for the next shoe to drop—or rather . . . the next body."

Chapter 2

As I step out of Lorraine's office, a weight lifts from my chest.

The memories of people dying aboard The Midnight Tide have always felt like a heavy burden. Now, somehow, that weight has eased—almost cut in half. Of course, it's not magic or some pseudoscience.

Like Lorraine said, it's about accepting what's beyond my control. When it comes to life and death, no one really holds the reins except a greater power.

It sounds like a simple truth—one I've always known deep down—but maybe hearing it from someone else makes it easier to swallow. Lorraine seems trustworthy. Someone who gets it.

I catch myself smiling at the thought, and Ben notices.

"You look lighter," he says with a smile. "Looks like you had a good session."

"I think she's great," I say, looping my arm around his waist.

He pulls me in, kissing the top of my head. "I'm already excited to see what comes next. When's your next appointment?"

"In two weeks," I tell him. "Right after our first cruise here."

"Right on schedule, then." His smile warms me, spreading through my chest like sunlight spilling over the horizon.

As we leave the building, Ben asks, "So, what do you want to do now? Any Miami sights on your list?"

I pause. Some quality time with Ben sounds good. But I know he's wiped out after steering The Midnight Tide into port and everything else.

I settle on something simpler. "How about we go grocery shopping?"

He raises an eyebrow. "Really? That'll make you feel better?"

I nod. "Absolutely. I want to cook for everyone tonight—you, Cole, Julia too."

His grin widens. "Julia will go on for days about how great a cook you are."

"Oh, you spoil me," I tease.

"Only because you deserve it."

We make our way to the grocery store. I stroll the aisles, Ben pushing the cart behind me, while my mind races through tonight's menu—a small thank-you for everyone. A way to honor all we've survived together.

After browsing the seafood section, I decide on seafood paella, with marinated olives, a mozzarella and tomato salad, and maybe a store-bought ciabatta.

I'd bake the bread myself if I had the time.

Ben trails close as I grab everything, then we argue playfully over wine—pinot gris or sauvignon blanc. I win, of course. It's my choice, after all, and Ben lets it slide.

As we head back to the parking lot, groceries in hand, I almost feel like we're married—imagining a future where our pantry is stocked and the kitchen smells like home.

Sweat beads on my forehead from the Miami heat, and I wonder—is it the air? The exercise? Or maybe Ben's steady support?

Stacy's constant love?

Julia's sunny optimism?

Cole's unwavering reliability?

Rex's loyal companionship?

It's all of it—combined.

For the rest of the afternoon, I catch myself smiling and humming. While Ben rests at his apartment, I get busy in the kitchen, prepping for tonight's dinner with everyone on the sixth floor invited.

As always, Stacy rifles through our moving boxes to find our matching aprons. She insists wearing them is mandatory for cooking together.

I would've said no, but when Stacy pulls out a tiny matching scarf for Rex, I can't say no.

So, the three of us—me, Stacy, and Rex—get to work. Rex entertains us with his antics, of course.

Before long, dinnertime arrives. Julia shows up first, wearing an olive-green dress with a matching cardigan. She even stopped by a bakery to bring apple pie.

Cole arrives next, then Ben.

Once we're all seated, the feast begins.

Ben leans close and whispers, "Let me guess—Julia's about to rave about how great a cook you are."

I chuckle. Sure enough, Julia exclaims, "Oh my, Rose! This food... it's amazing!"

Ben snorts right on cue.

Stacy clears her throat. "Hey Julia, I chopped the ingredients and seasoned everything, just so you know."

Cole chuckles, shaking his head. "Do you really need credit for that?"

Ben and I laugh, soaking in the warmth and laughter around the table.

Halfway through, Stacy shifts the conversation while munching her salad. "So, this new route—Miami to San Juan, right? What's waiting for us onboard? I already booked a ticket, by the way."

I wave my fork. "And you got a discount."

Stacy laughs. "How else would I afford all these cruises? Seriously though, as a guest, what should I expect besides the new ocean views? The Dutchman Cruise and The Grand Weaver were already amazing. What's this one called?"

Julia answers, smiling, "The Emerald Isles."

Stacy winks. "Right. So, what's the buzz on The Emerald Isles cruise by The Midnight Tide?"

I joke, "Lots of dancers in bikinis."

Stacy rolls her eyes. "No fun."

Ben wipes his mouth and chimes in, "If you must know, Stacy, we're holding the very first poker tournament onboard. We're setting up a brand-new casino as we speak."

Stacy blanks for a moment, then blurts, "Really? A casino?"

Ben shoots her a half-concerned, half-amused look. "What? You don't like it?"

"I mean... I don't know poker at all," Stacy shrugs.

"I can teach you," Cole offers right away, ever the trusty boyfriend.

Stacy squeezes Cole's hand briefly. "Well, we still have a few days before the cruise, right? We can do whatever we want here in Miami."

The rest of the dinner moves along smoothly.

Eventually, the conversation drifts to our previous cruises on The Midnight Tide. You can feel it in the air—everyone tiptoes around the topic of the murders we solved and survived.

Though I've gained a more positive outlook on those dark days, I can't stop the tightening in my chest whenever that unspoken topic looms.

Julia breaks the silence by mentioning some of our eccentric guests from past voyages—like the woman who carried a collection of unusual purses, including a watermelon replica and a bagel with a strap.

Cole jumps in with a story about escorting a guest back to his room because he refused to take off his full snorkeling gear—even in the dining hall. Mask, snorkel, fins, the whole package.

I laugh sincerely at the stories... for a moment.

Then the voices around me start to fade, like I'm hearing them underwater.

Rex nudges my leg, snapping me back to the present.

"Healing from trauma isn't a straight line, Rose." That's what Lorraine told me today. So it's okay to feel like this sometimes.

As fast as I dive into my cocoon of misery, I pull myself back into the happy circle again.

After the dishes are cleared, Stacy spreads out her grazing board. And yes, we open the first of three bottles of that sauvignon blanc Ben and I picked out.

Sitting together, swapping stories and laughter, it's easy to forget the memories that usually choke me awake at night.

Even as I'm working through it with a therapist, I know the memories are still there. But this time, I'm confident things will get better.

Outside, the stars seem brighter, as if the ocean reflects their glow and amplifies it across the city.

By quarter to midnight, Julia's out cold at the table, head resting on folded arms, still clutching a half-eaten grape.

Since Stacy and Cole linger on the balcony, I tell Ben, "Let's get Julia to her apartment. She'll be more comfortable there."

Ben, wiping down glasses, nods. "Of course. Let me put these away first."

Like the gentleman he is, Ben quickly dries and puts away the wine glasses. Then he rolls down his sleeves. "Okay, I'm ready."

I crouch beside Julia, trying to rouse her. "Julia? Hey, time to head back."

She shifts her head and groans but doesn't sit up.

I chuckle. "I don't think she can walk on her own."

"No worries. We'll just carry her," Ben offers.

I pull Julia upright and lean her weight on Ben. He loops one of her arms over his shoulder. "Okay, we're good."

I grab Julia's bag before we head out. In the hallway, I find her apartment key, unlock the door, and we step inside.

Instantly, I'm taken by how Julia's bright touches transform the space.

"Wow," I whisper, taking in the red, orange, and yellow throw pillows on the couch and a purplish-blue hydrangea resting on the dining table. "She's already made it her own."

Ben nods, impressed. "That's something."

Julia mumbles something unintelligible as we carry her toward the bedroom, which is just as colorful. Her bedding's a soft pink, with pillows and a blanket in deeper fuchsia tones.

We carefully lay her down. Ben excuses himself so I can peel off her shoes and cardigan, then tuck her under the covers.

It takes some effort, and by the end, sweat clings to my back. Still, it's worth it when Julia weakly grabs my arm and whispers, "I like you a lot, Rose."

I laugh, touched by her innocence. On my way out, I smile and say, "I like you a lot, too."

Once she's settled, I find Ben waiting in the hallway. I close the door behind me and turn to him.

"Thanks for helping carry her."

He gestures toward my apartment at the other end of the hall. "It was, what, fifty steps? No big deal."

I squint down the hallway. "I'm sure it's more than that."

Ben takes my hand. "Want to check out the rooftop with me? I saw it earlier and figured it'd be better in the evening."

"Yeah, let's go."

We walk to the stairs and climb up. Seconds later, we're under a canopy of endless twinkling stars.

The rooftop terrace gleams atop the building. The air smells salty, mixed with sunscreen and the city's pulse. Below, Ocean Drive buzzes with Miami nightlife. Neon signs flicker across the street, and distant Latin music pulses from nearby clubs.

A weathered bench glimmers under solar-powered fairy lights. In one corner, there's a small vegetable garden—or an attempt at one.

It's breathtaking.

"Wow." I inhale the humid air. "I didn't expect Miami to be... sentimental."

Ben leans on the railing. "Sentimental?"

"You know. Like a postcard you glance at sometimes—a snapshot of Miami frozen in time. But even in the photo, you can taste the ocean... and sweat."

Ben laughs. "Odd description for Miami, but I like it. It is a beautiful city."

"I agree." I nod slowly, soaking it all in. It's impressive how alive the city still feels, even past midnight.

For a moment, we're quiet, just soaking in the moment.

Then Ben breaks the silence. "You know, I'm a little nervous about this new route. Excited, sure—but nervous, too."

Hearing that, I step closer to Ben and stand beside him, leaning my chin on his bicep as I look up at him. This is one of the many things I love about Ben—his raw honesty, something he used to hold back from me.

I say, "It's okay to be nervous about new things, right?"

Ben brushes his index finger lightly on the tip of my nose. "I know. I just want things to be perfect this time. That's all."

"You mean... incident-free?" I ask, my voice cautious.

"If it can be," he hopes, eyes drifting up to the stars as if making a silent wish.

In that moment, I wish I could promise Ben everything will be perfect—at least incident-free. But that's not really up to me, or to him, just like Lorraine said.

Still, I want to ease his mind the way he always does for me.

So I wrap my arms around his waist and hug him.

Even though I don't know what's waiting for us on this new cruise—and yes, I'm nervous, too—I say, "We'll try our best to keep the cruise perfect, okay?"

Chapter 3
Four Days Before the Incident

The Port of Miami is a feast for the senses—buzzing with life and noise: engines humming rhythmically, seagulls screeching overhead, and the distant rumble of cargo operations.

Before us, The Midnight Tide gleams under the bright Florida sun, mighty and proud. Just below, crew members wait for us to arrive.

Today, Ben's meeting with some of them about our upcoming cruise, The Emerald Isles.

I spot Ben chatting with the head engineer; his first mate stands close by. He and Cole went ahead earlier this morning, so it's just Julia and me making our way toward them.

"This sunlight is killing me," Julia groans beside me, shielding her eyes with a hand like her dark sunglasses aren't quite cutting it.

I glance over, amused. For once, her blouse and skirt don't match. I tease, "That's because you have a hangover."

She groans again. "I can't believe I embarrassed myself last night. I'm so sorry, Rose!"

I laugh, sliding my arm through hers. "Come on, Julia. Lighten up. Ben and I just had to drag you across the hallway to get you to bed."

She claps her hands over her ears and winces, clearly mortified she only fell asleep after her sixth glass of wine. It wasn't that bad. Still, she pleads, "Please don't tell me more!"

"Okay, ladies, you okay there?" Ben calls out as we approach.

Julia lowers her hands and straightens up, professional as ever. She greets with a sing-song lilt, "Good morning, Captain. Everyone..."

"Good morning," I add with a soft smile.

The group murmurs their greetings as we join them.

Ben counts heads. "Looks like we have everyone we need. Should we start the meeting?"

The crew nods and murmurs agreement.

Ben gets started. "As you may know, we're launching a new route for The Midnight Tide cruises—The Emerald Isles. Nine days from Miami to San Juan."

His first mate hands him a clipboard, which Ben quickly scans. "From Miami, we'll sail to Amber Cove on day three, Basseterre on day five, then St. Lucia, Dominica, St. Maarten, and finally San Juan."

He returns the clipboard. "The route's new, but so is an amenity: our casino, currently under construction. It's on track to be finished a day before the cruise. Very exciting."

We can't help but clap and cheer at the news.

Ben continues, "Thanks to a major sponsorship, we're hosting our very first annual poker game exclusive to this cruise. High rollers on board, and as always, I expect stellar service from all of us."

He happily claps his hands. "Anyone want to see the casino's progress?"

Everyone murmurs agreement, and we follow Ben up the gangway. It's like an inspection day, but this time, just for the casino.

Julia leans in behind me as we walk. "I saw the pending guest list from the company. There's an interesting name."

I glance back. "Yeah? Who?"

"Jasper Thorne."

We enter the ship's reception area before I reply. "Sounds like you expect me to know him."

Julia taps her forehead lightly. "Wrong to expect that. He's a famous poker player—one of the biggest. He's joining us."

"So, we're excited to have him aboard," I say flatly, following the crowd. Ben's voice drones on, chatting with the crew.

Julia tilts her head uncertainly, searching for words. "I'm not sure 'excited' fits Jasper Thorne."

"What's that supposed to mean?"

"It means Jasper's problematic—wrapped up in controversies. His moral compass is... defective, if it works at all."

We cross the atrium, passing the grand staircase, then the so-called shopper's lane: souvenir, clothes, swimwear, and convenience stores—all closed and nearly empty for now.

I shoot Julia a concerned look. "Heavy accusation, Jules."

"But it's not an accusation," Julia insists firmly. "I've read plenty about him. Trouble follows wherever he goes."

I shake off the thought. "Well, don't jinx it."

Julia backpedals. "I'll keep an eye on him, promise."

I chuckle at Julia's attempt to reassure me. The nightmares have been bad lately, but my care team helps me get through.

I nudge Julia teasingly as we reach the casino hallway. "You better make sure Jasper Thorne doesn't cause problems."

Ben's voice echoes ahead. "Here we are."

Behind him, The Midnight Tide's casino buzzes with activity, still under construction. The smell of sawdust, fresh paint, and coffee fills the air.

Power tools whir. Hammers strike nails. Workers shout instructions. Electricians string cables. Painters roll fresh coats. The room hums with purpose.

Despite scaffolding and plastic-covered gaming tables, the dazzling casino floor shines through. Chandeliers hang ready to light. Anticipation thickens the air.

"As you can see," Ben explains, "construction's nearly finished. On cruise day, we officially open this casino and welcome our high rollers for the first annual poker tournament."

Applause rises from the group.

After a quick tour of the new casino, Julia and I break away from the group and head to our shared office on the ship's lower level.

Our office isn't big, but it has everything we need: two desks, swiveling chairs, two computers, a printer, a metal cabinet, and a window looking out at the endless ocean.

We settle at our desks to start planning the schedule for the upcoming nine-day cruise.

So far, all we have locked in is the poker tournament. That's it.

Thankfully, Julia's already been brainstorming ideas even before today's meeting.

"Since this is a Caribbean cruise, we should have summery events," Julia says. "Like family-friendly movie nights by the pool, maybe a bubble show for the kids."

My eyes light up at the suggestions. "That's perfect. Movie nights every evening by the pool. An outdoor cinema setup, different movies each night."

Julia pulls out her notebook and scribbles fast. "I'll make a list of family-friendly movies. Maybe morning reruns for anyone who missed the night before?"

"Sounds great," I say. "For the bubble show, how about the morning of day two? And a fire performance on night three. If you can find someone who can join us by then."

Julia nods, writing furiously as I toss out ideas.

"For night five in Basseterre, St. Kitts—did you know they have a jazz festival there? We could book a small jazz performance in the dining hall."

"Ooh, that sounds fun!" Julia beams. "And since the itinerary hits a bunch of Caribbean islands later, a pyro show between stops would be amazing. Guys dancing with balls of flame. Perfect, Rose!"

I raise a finger to clarify, "Outdoors only. And fire safety pros on standby."

"Noted," Julia agrees without missing a beat.

I see it in her eyes—she's already mapping out who to call first, where to host each event, how to make it all work.

Having Julia's brain and drive on my team is a lifesaver as cruise director.

For hours, we hammer out the schedule—movie nights, bubble show, jazz, pyro, and even a treasure hunt. Ten souvenirs hidden around the ship, each with a prize when found. Interactive and perfectly Caribbean-themed. I'm genuinely excited.

After printing the schedule, I leave Julia to make her calls and hunt down Ben for approval.

Finding him isn't hard—he's on the bridge, tinkering with equipment and tech, even though inspection day's still days away.

I knock lightly at the doorway. "Knock, knock."

Ben looks up from the electronic chart display. "Hey, Rose. Just finished the crew meeting. We'll regroup here the day before the cruise for—"

"Inspection," I finish, stepping inside. The bridge feels emptier than usual. I spin in one of the chairs facing the navigation systems.

Ben chuckles. "So, what brings you here? Missing me?"

I roll my eyes. "That's not exactly how you talk to your cruise director, Captain."

He pulls a chair close. "Well, this cruise director just happens to be the love of my life."

I make a silly face. "Please don't say that out loud in public."

He throws his head back, laughing. "Fine, I'm sorry. I can get romantic sometimes."

"Well, don't," I snap back, grinning. Then I hand him the schedule. "Anyway, I'm here for your approval. If you're good with it, we'll finalize and send out emails to guests about what to expect."

Ben flips through the pages, eyes scanning carefully. He nods. "Looks good. You're taking precautions for the pyro show, right?"

"Absolutely. Julia's making calls as we speak."

"Then it's all good." He hands the folder back.

I nod and stand, but pause. "Hey, did you hear about Jasper Thorne? One of the high rollers for the poker tournament?"

Ben's expression tightens just slightly. "I've heard a few things."

I hesitate but press on, seeking reassurance. "You don't think he'll cause us... problems, do you?"

Ben squeezes my hand, just like he always does, rubbing his thumb gently. "If he does, we'll handle it. We always do."

He's right, but I still can't shake this uneasy feeling deep in my gut.

Chapter 4
Thirteen Hours Before the Incident

"Is everything ready?" Ben—well, Captain Anderson—stands in the doorway of the newly furnished casino, sharp in his crisp white uniform. His hair is meticulously styled with wax, and his cologne cuts through the lingering smell of fresh paint.

I stand just behind him, wearing a sharp suit and pencil skirt, my gold-plated name tag shining with my name and position. Above it, the ship's logo gleams from a pin shaped like the Midnight Tide itself.

By my side, Rex proudly scans the room, briefly distracted by the buzzing lights and sounds. Even he's in uniform—a tiny vest matching the employees' colors. Stacy isn't the only honorary crew member on this ship.

The casino manager, Jude Romero, hurries to the door to greet Ben. "Captain Anderson, good morning. As you can see, everything's in order here at the casino."

I sweep my eyes across the room, sunlight pouring through the glass wall and reflecting off polished marble and gleaming chrome. Outside, the Atlantic Ocean stretches endless and calm.

Rows of slot machines sit on standby, their screens flashing inviting colors and music. The gaming tables are immaculate, their felt surfaces untouched—the only thing missing is the players.

Soon, this place will thrum with energy—people at every machine, drawn by the lure of the game, or more specifically, the thrill of winning.

"And the tournament?" Ben asks, eyes flicking toward the poker tables arranged neatly on one side.

Jude's smile broadens. "All set, Captain. You don't have to worry about a thing."

Not even Jasper Thorne?

The thought sneaks into my head before I can stop it.

I swallow it down and stay silent.

Jude's confidence eases even Ben's slight tension. Checking his watch, Ben notes we have five minutes until doors open to guests. "I'm glad everything's going smoothly here. Don't forget to contact Miss Dela Cruz if anything comes up, alright?"

"Absolutely," Jude replies, flashing a friendly smile in my direction.

I return it, but my mind lingers elsewhere.

Ben leans in, voice low. "We better get to the entrance."

"Right behind you," I mumble, pressing my two-inch heels against the floor as we move out.

Ben, Rex, and I hurry toward the ship's main entrance.

Crew members buzz around, finishing last-minute preparations, their energy electrifying the ship.

Outside, the panoramic windows frame Miami's skyline to the left, the endless ocean to the right, its surface rippling with the ship's gentle motion.

The sight, the salty air, the hum of engines beneath my feet—they all remind me that we're back on the water, back to work. Excitement and nerves swirl inside me.

As always, we line up above the gangway, ready to welcome the guests.

Rex stands near Julia, a few people ahead of me. Ben and I linger at the front, poised.

His first mate radios port staff to confirm all systems are go. When the signal comes through, Ben radios back, "Open the gates."

And in they stream.

We greet each guest with practiced smiles, guiding VIPs to their suites. It's a routine I secretly savor—catching up with returning passengers and meeting new ones.

Usually, the ship departs within thirty minutes, but at 8:31 a.m., after escorting another VIP to their room, I notice something off—the announcement from the bridge isn't playing through the speakers.

Picking up my radio, I call out, "Charlie to Alpha. Is everything okay? Why aren't we embarking?"

Static crackles before Ben's voice comes through. "We're waiting on a passenger running late... Actually, he's boarding now. We'll leave any minute."

Who's the guest holding us up?

I'm curious but hold the question.

Drawn toward the entrance, I see the crew detaching the gangway and closing the door.

No important guest in sight.

I make my way to the reception, where Stacy happens to be standing.

"There you are! Found you bright and early," she says, beaming. Usually, I don't spot her until hours into the cruise.

I grin back. "Great. You can keep me company while I do my inspection. But first…"

I approach the receptionist behind the information desk. "Excuse me, which guest was running late just now?"

She glances at her computer. "Mr. Jasper Thorne."

Just then, the announcement music floods the speakers.

"Good morning, ladies and gentlemen. This is Captain Ben Anderson speaking. We are pleased to announce that The Emerald Isles Cruise by The Midnight Tide is now ready to depart en route to San Juan. For hassle-free travel, please ensure all your belongings are secure and all your rooms are closed. We wish you a safe, enjoyable, and unforgettable voyage with us."

The announcement ends. The ship hums and creaks as it slowly pulls away from Miami's port.

Beside me, Stacy giggles with excitement. "Here we go, Caribbean!"

"Here we go, indeed," a voice calls out behind her.

A guy with blond hair tied back into a 'manly' bun approaches, eyes scanning Stacy from head to toe.

"I knew I'd find you on this cruise."

Stacy blinks, confused. "I'm sorry, but do we know each other?"

"Not yet," he says breezily, extending his hand. "I'm Jasper Thorne, and you are... the woman of my dreams."

Stacy's face twists in disgust at the cheesy pickup line.

A chill runs down my spine as I finally put a face to the troublesome Jasper Thorne.

Stacy ignores the handshake, clearly not wanting any kind of physical contact with the otherwise creepy guy. Jasper just saw Stacy—her undeniable beauty, of course—and decided to swagger over with his usual cocky attitude.

Stacy replies, "Uh, cool, but I'm... married, yeah. And before you ask about my ring, it's in my room. I kept it there because I didn't want to lose it on this cruise. So..."

"Well, hold on." Jasper chuckles, and even that sound grates on my nerves. "If I were your husband, you could lose as many rings as you wanted, and I'd just buy you more."

"Well, you're not my husband, so if you'll excuse us..." Stacy starts wrapping her arms around mine, ready to make a break for it.

But before she can pull me away, Jasper's eyes catch my name tag. "Oh, cruise director?" His gaze lifts from the tag to my face, and somehow his expression brightens. "Didn't see you there, Rose."

I can tell he's shifting focus now, since Stacy isn't taking the bait. Unlike her, I can't afford to be rude without cause, so I force a polite smile. "Good morning, Mr. Thorne. I'm sure you don't want us keeping you from your vacation. I was just assisting a guest. We'll get going if you don't need anything else."

"I need something from you," Jasper says fast. I've only known him a few minutes, but I already feel his irritation settling in under my skin.

With a steady smile, I ask, "What is it, Mr. Thorne?"

"A... tour!" He improvises on the spot. "You're the cruise director, right? You can give me an exclusive tour. I don't mind being seen walking with you."

Hearing that, Stacy, my ever-watchful sister, jumps in to protect me. "You know what? Rose was about to give me a tour too. You can just tag along. I personally know the head of security—I can have him assist us instead. I'm sure Rose is very busy. What do you think?"

Jasper runs a hand through his perfectly styled hair and mumbles, "Sounds… less fun, so I'll pass." But he doesn't miss the chance to wink at me as he walks off. "Rain check on that tour? See you around."

Just like that, he drifts away from the reception, eyes scanning the near-empty floor for his next target. I already have reason to worry about him.

"That's absolutely creepy," Stacy says once he's out of sight.

I keep watching his shadow vanish down the hall. "I was told I'd have to keep an eye on that guy."

"Really?" Stacy sounds surprised. She's no poker fan and doesn't know Jasper. "Why? Does he have a criminal record or something?"

"God, I hope not," I admit, suddenly worried I didn't check. Maybe I should have. "But I was told trouble is his middle name."

"Are you sure it's not 'creep'?"

"That might be his other middle name—I can't tell."

Stacy laughs.

Though we joke, a chill creeps over me, sinking into my skin like expired lotion gone wrong, making me burn with unease.

What kind of problems will Jasper bring us?

Whatever it is, I just hope it doesn't involve blood—or worse, a dead body.

Chapter 5
Two Hours Before the Incident

The casino buzzes with an anticipatory energy—well, "buzz" barely scratches the surface. The entire room vibrates with overlapping noises: chatter, laughter, instrumental music drifting softly from hidden speakers, slot machines chiming their relentless jingles, Russian roulette balls clattering in their cylinders, cards shuffling, and chips clinking sharply against the green felt tables.

Inside, the usual metal creaks of the ship and the ocean's distant roar are swallowed by the cacophony, like the sea itself is holding its breath beneath this electric atmosphere.

On the far side of the room—where the high-stakes poker tournament will unfold—a sleek table stands polished and ready. A professional dealer watches over it with practiced calm. Cameras are set up for the live feed streaming to online viewers, microphones are discreetly placed to catch every whisper, and high-definition screens hang overhead, glowing with anticipation.

Julia's eyes flicker around the room, scanning from corner to corner with mechanical precision. I can sense her nerves—though she hides it well. But really, she's just mirroring mine. I try to convince myself I'm calm, but my palms are slick, and my throat tightens.

Rex stands alert at my feet, his body tense, eyes sharp. It's like he knows something's off, something I can't quite put my finger on. Protective as ever, he seems ready to shield me from whatever trouble's simmering beneath this glittering surface.

Because that's exactly how it feels—this tournament isn't just a game. Something deeper, unseen, is weaving its threads through the air, tightening with every passing second.

Players start trickling in, their faces all too familiar. Four of them—veterans, by the look of it—chat their way to the table, aided by Jude, the casino manager, who nods in recognition as he ushers them in.

Julia whispers beside me, ticking off names and tidbits. "That guy's a poker legend." "His brother's some kind of celebrity." "That one? Million-dollar business owner." The roster reads like a who's who of power and wealth.

As the seats fill, my eyes dart repeatedly to the entrance. Jasper Thorne isn't here yet. If he's missing, trouble's probably brewing somewhere else on this ship.

So, I wait.

The clock ticks closer to 9:00 PM... and still, no Jasper.

Jude glances nervously toward the international clocks mounted on the far wall. I watch the second hand on my wristwatch tick—tick, tock, tick, tock—each beat louder than the last in my head.

Players grumble, restless murmurs rising as the last competitor finally takes his place moments before the official start. I reach for my radio, about to call Jasper's name, when he finally strides into the casino—swaggering in like he owns the place, arrogance trailing behind him like a shadow.

Rex growls low and quiet, but loud enough to slice through the din. It's not like him to bark here, especially while we're working. I crouch, pressing a hand against his head. "Easy, bud. No need to growl, okay?"

Rex settles, sitting but still locked on Jasper.

"Mr. Thorne!" Jude hurries over, sweat beading on his brow. "The players have been waiting. Please, take your seat—"

Jasper tosses his leather jacket over the chair and slides in, his grin met by scowls and shaking heads. "Relax, folks. It's not like I kept you waiting for an hour. Two minutes late, tops. If you're so twitchy, let's get this show on the road. I'm here to win."

His blond hair falls past his shoulders, almost knightly against his bushy brows—a medieval rogue transplanted into a high-stakes poker game.

The table's disapproval only grows; no one here likes him. Honestly, I don't blame them. He's hard to tolerate.

Julia leans close and murmurs, "He's definitely... a character."

"You can say that again," I reply, eyes drifting to Jude, who clears his throat and announces the start of The Midnight Tide's inaugural poker tournament. He keeps it brief, knowing the players' patience is thin and time is tight.

The game begins. A hush falls over the room as the dealer slides cards across the table.

Julia, Rex, and I stand at the sidelines, watching the players and the swelling crowd circle the table like sharks. Faces shift—stoic, cold, calculating.

The players barely glance at their cards, hiding their hands, keeping every move locked behind carefully controlled expressions. These are pros.

Jasper, however, doesn't wipe the smirk from his face even as he folds on the first round.

The game moves forward.

Out of the corner of my eye, I spot a blonde woman trailing behind Jasper, her gaze sharp and burning. She sips a frozen margarita, leaving a lipstick stain on the glass's rim. Her glare drills into the back of Jasper's head—charged, deliberate. I can't shake the feeling it's hatred.

Julia notices my stare. "Jasper's a known womanizer. I wouldn't be shocked if she's a scorned ex."

"Huh," I say flatly, noting the woman's styled curls and the beauty mark just above her lip. "Looks the part."

"Definitely," Julia agrees.

I refocus on the game, watching every flick of the dealer's wrist, every chip pushed forward, every subtle twitch in the players' faces—all except Jasper, who either smirks or chuckles quietly to himself.

Players fold, check, bluff, and counter-bluff—each move a calculated risk, some gambled on pure luck. The stakes climb, money flowing like it's play money, though thousands are on the line.

The tension builds.

An hour passes.

All ten players remain, but the careful restraint from earlier is gone. A man suddenly pushes his entire stack of chips forward.

"All in," he declares, voice sharp and steady.

The next player hesitates, then matches him, sliding all his chips into the pile.

Julia exhales sharply beside me. "They've got enough chips here to buy an island!"

If only I understood the game.

I nod, folding my arms across my chest.

More players push chips forward, the pile growing—enough to buy two islands now. Only two players fold.

Jasper's the last to make a move, and the room holds its breath.

This time, his smirk blooms into a grin so wide and wild, it reminds me of the Joker.

He nudges his tower of chips forward, watching with smug satisfaction as they topple into the center. "All in."

The crowd gasps, whispers swirling in disbelief. This has to be the final hand.

Eight players at the table—four jittery, three passive, and Jasper, grinning like a psychopath. I can almost guess how this ends.

The dealer flips the community cards one by one: a king, then an ace, and finally a queen.

Silence crashes over the room, thick with nervous anticipation.

I barely know poker, but one thing I do know: a royal flush. If a player holds a ten and a jack, they've got the unbeatable hand.

Odds are slim—eight players to one. In a fifty-two card deck, the chance is... less than one percent.

Even I'm impressed I did that math in my head, though I'm sure the decimal's off.

Now the community cards lay bare, and frustration floods half the players who went all in. At least five curse, toss their cards, and storm out mid-tournament. Thousands of dollars lost.

Jasper bursts into laughter, ignoring protocol as he slaps his cards on the table—an ace and a jack. The royal flush.

Before anyone can react, Jasper springs to his feet, dancing and jumping.

He won.

A businessman slams his fist on the table. "No way! Tell me how you cheated this time, you prick!"

Jasper doesn't hear him. He's cheering, still dancing, and grabs Jude to plant a kiss on his cheek. "Take all those chips to the cashier's cage. I want my money in paper bills."

Without a backward glance, Jasper hops away from the table, leaving a trail of angry stares.

Another player grunts, "He cheated, didn't he?"

"Of course he did!" someone else snaps. "Why was he even allowed to play? Doesn't he cheat all the time?"

Jude, wiping sweat from his brow, signals an employee who starts gathering Jasper's chips into a bag.

Jude raises his hands. "Sirs, please calm down—"

"Screw that." The businessman kicks his chair aside and storms off. "Like anyone's going to investigate. Jasper probably bought everyone on this damn cruise to let him win!"

Others grumble their agreement.

Watching the angry mob exit, I keep my eyes on Jasper by the cashier's cage, worried someone might jump him as he exchanges chips for cash.

Their glares and insults trail after him, but they leave. I step over to Jude. "You should look into these accusations. We don't want a mutiny on the ship."

Jude nods, visibly tense. "I should, shouldn't I?"

I give his back a reassuring pat. "Thanks, Jude. Keep me posted."

"He's leaving." Julia tugs my sleeve, spotting Jasper pulling another black duffel from the cashier's cage—the night's haul. "Should we follow him?"

I glance at Jude one last time, then back at Julia. "I want to question him about his luck, but maybe you should stay and help Jude with this... cheating mess."

Julia hesitates, then hands me Rex's leash.

Rex and I tail Jasper out of the casino, the weight of that bag heavy on his arm. While Jude probes the accusations, I plan to confront Jasper directly—no use skirting the issue.

We hurry out, my eyes locked on Jasper's back, determined to catch any sign of trickery.

But as we cross the threshold, a woman blocks our path. "You're casino staff, right?"

I shift my gaze between her and Jasper. "Uh, yes... can we help you?"

"My son," she says urgently, gripping my arm. "He's lost in the crowd. He's only five. Please, can you help me find him?"

Jasper vanishes down the hallway.

I want to pull away, but I can't ignore her worry—etched deeply across her face.

Rex looks up at me, silently asking what to do.

I say, "Of course. Where did you last see him?"

My gut says Jasper needs my attention, but my heart won't let me turn away.

Jasper will have to wait.

Despite the nagging unease pulling me back toward him, we start searching for the boy.

It doesn't take long. Rex leads us to the promenade deck, where a little boy plays with a toy car, oblivious.

"Oh, thank goodness!" the mother scoops him up, relief flooding her voice. "Thank you so much!"

"You're welcome." I offer a smile.

Glancing at my watch, I realize we only lost ten minutes with Jasper. I excuse myself, leash in hand, heading back inside.

Then my phone buzzes in my pocket.

I pull it out. Caller ID: Mrs. Abernathy. A returning passenger in one of the presidential suites.

Why call at a quarter past eleven?

"Hello, Mrs. Abernathy?" My heart skips. "Is everything alright?"

"Oh, Rose! So glad you're awake!" she rushes. "I think I need security up here in the presidential suites!"

"What's going on? Did something happen?" I feel Rex's gaze on me.

"There's a commotion on the upper decks! I can hear it!"

I freeze.

A commotion?

Oh, no.

Chapter 6
Ten Minutes After the Incident

"What is it?" Cole asks, eyes fixed on Jasper's body, just a couple of feet away. His face twists—not just discomfort but something deeper. Anxiety, fear, exhaustion—etched into every line. His teeth grit beneath a heavy frown, and the deep crease between his furrowed brows is impossible to miss.

I feel all those emotions too, swirling inside me, tangled up with the endless questions pounding through my mind. What happened? Who did this? Why is it happening again?

Therapy's taught me not to shoulder the blame, not to drown in guilt when tragedy strikes. But even so, I can't stop wondering... if I had followed Jasper more closely, could I have stopped this?

Could one five-minute conversation have kept him from walking straight into his own murder?

Cole still looks queasy, but Ben steps forward, crouching beside Jasper. "Gold poker chips. We don't use those in the casino."

"I noticed that," I say, swallowing hard against the lump rising in my throat—threatening to choke or silence me any second now. "I watched the entire tournament. No gold chips in sight. Only green, black, purple, and... yellow. That's the gold."

"So if they're not ours, who put them on a dead man?" Cole asks.

"The killer," I say flatly.

Ben, Cole, and Rex all turn to me at once, their faces registering surprise at how cold I sound. I didn't mean it that way... but maybe indifference is my armor now. Could detachment help me survive this? Or is that just another way to bury the guilt?

Before I can get lost in that thought, I ask, "DIY forensic kit?"

Cole backs out to the living room and returns with the familiar black case—packed with gloves, fingerprint powders, tape, evidence bags, brushes, and luminol. Experience has its ugly perks. Murder on this ship isn't new to us.

I don't take pride in knowing the drill, but I slip on latex gloves with steady hands, grab the camera, and start shooting the scene before disturbing anything.

Cole and Ben fall in behind me.

Cole snaps photos, numbering each piece of evidence as he places small plastic markers. Ben dons gloves and scrutinizes every inch with those sharp eyes.

We don't speak while working—only when we finish bagging and tagging everything, even the gold chips lying over Jasper's closed eyes, making him look like he's just asleep.

By now, it's past midnight.

Cole breaks the silence. "Robbery gone wrong, maybe? You said he left the casino with a bag full of cash, right, Rose?"

"I thought that too," I say, not taking my eyes off Jasper's peaceful, staged expression. "But they didn't just take the money and 'accidentally' kill him. They put gold chips over his eyes, like a message."

From the corner of my eye, I catch Ben pulling out his phone, scrolling fast. "Internet says gold chips mean $1,000 denominations. Maybe no symbolic meaning. Maybe... payment for Jasper's life?"

Cole wrinkles his nose. "If they're robbers, and the chips are worth that much, why leave them behind? They want the money."

"Maybe not the money," I say without much conviction. Honestly, my brain feels numb. "What if it's just Jasper's life? Taking the money could be a distraction, a setup to throw off investigators from the real motive."

Ben and Cole nod, but Ben's hesitation lingers. "Maybe we shouldn't get tangled in theories. It's too soon to know. What we do know is someone on this ship wanted Jasper dead."

"But who?" Cole mutters.

I bite my cheek before answering, "That's tough. Tonight alone, I saw nine or ten people glaring at him. Didn't you hear? The guy's a menace."

"Well, we still have eight days to figure out which one pulled the trigger," Ben says.

A sharp knock at the door makes me flinch—an unwelcome jolt that cracks the fragile calm I tried to fake.

Cole reassures me. "It's Dr. Bates. I asked him to join us."

Yeah, we're methodical like that. Professionals.

Still, beneath the surface, I can't shake the gnawing feeling that Jasper's death is partly on me.

I should've followed him. No matter what.

Rex rubs his head against my leg, sensing my shift in mood. That dog always knows. If he weren't the amazing companion he is, I might call it supernatural. But Rex is my rock.

I crouch to scratch behind his ears just as Dr. Bates enters, carrying his medical bag. His thinning white hair and thicker glasses speak of years, but he moves with unwavering purpose.

Seeing Jasper sprawled on the floor, Dr. Bates clicks his tongue four times. "First night of the cruise, always the first night. Who is it this time?"

He kneels next to the body and immediately gets to work.

Neither Ben nor Cole answers, so I fill the silence. "Jasper Thorne. Professional poker player. He was at tonight's tournament."

Dr. Bates squints at Jasper. "Ah, the smug one. Watched the live feed from the morgue. His overconfidence finally caught up with him. Literally."

"Took his life, too," I sigh.

"Now, now, Miss Dela Cruz," Dr. Bates chides gently, inspecting the body. "Don't take it personally. I've been a medical examiner a long time. If I looked at every dead body the way you do, I'd lose my mind."

"How'd you know I—" I stop, words failing me. It's complicated, this constant dance with death aboard the ship.

Dr. Bates chuckles—a sound I couldn't manage if I were unbuttoning a dead man's undershirt after unzipping his leather jacket. "We've worked together a long time, Miss Dela Cruz. You always have the same look in your eyes when we face this kind of thing. Tell you what—"

He pauses, gloved hand folding back Jasper's collar. A purplish-black bruise rings Jasper's neck, the clear imprint of a rope or cord.

"Strangulation," Dr. Bates says, shifting from fatherly to clinical. "This bruising happens when enough external force is applied around the neck. I'll need to confirm back at the morgue if that's the cause of death...but that's what it looks like right now."

My breath catches, the lump in my throat finally swallowing my voice whole. I can't speak. Words lodge in my closed throat.

As Dr. Bates pulls back, Cole offers to call his contact to bring the body bag.

What happens next blurs into a haze, like wading through thick, blinding fog. I catch fragments.

Cole orders his team to clear the hallway first. Two security guards wheel in a stretcher and body bag. I think they ask me to step back, but when I don't move, Ben gently pulls me aside, voice barely a whisper, "Are you okay?"

The fog dulls my sight and hearing.

Then—Stacy's shaking me awake. "Rose? Rose? Are you okay? Hey! Look at me!"

Her voice cuts through the trance. I snap back, still sitting on Jasper's living room couch. "Stacy? What are you doing here?"

"I called her," Ben says, eyes worried, eyebrows knit tight. "You were... out of it for a bit."

"A bit?" Stacy repeats, gripping my hand like she's afraid to lose me. "You were dissociating for half an hour, Rose!"

I want to deny it, but that's exactly what happened. Still, I lift a shaky smile at the worried faces around me. "I'm sorry. I'm fine now. I just... lost my head for a moment back there."

"That's never happened before, right?" Stacy asks carefully.

Behind her, Ben adds, "If this is too much, maybe we should—"

"No, Ben," I cut in firmly, pushing myself up from the couch. "I'm fine, really. It was just momentary."

"Yeah, Rose, but—"

I stop Stacy before she speaks. "Look, I just... I can't help but blame myself this time, okay?"

I decide to be honest. They need the truth. I need them.

"I'm more aware of my feelings now. I get why I react the way I do. But today... I could've stopped Jasper from dying. I was supposed to follow him after the tournament to talk, but I was ten minutes too late. So I feel guilty. If only I'd—"

Before I finish, Ben wraps me in a tight hug. Doesn't care Stacy's on the couch or Cole's watching from the doorway. He just holds me.

"It's not your fault, Rose. Don't ever let yourself think that again. You hear me?"

I pull back gently, tears gathering but held back. "I guess I just needed a reminder."

Ben kisses the top of my head. "Remember that."

Stacy's hand finds my back with a comforting squeeze. "You should stay in my suite tonight. What do you think?"

I don't hesitate. "That sounds great, Stace."

But though it sounds good, I don't feel good. My body feels like it's melting away, held together only by my skin.

Still, I know I have to hold it together tonight... because this is only the beginning of Jasper's end.

Chapter 7

Stacy and I walk arm-in-arm back to her deluxe suite, just one deck down from the presidential suites.

Instead of grabbing her usual remedy for everything—wine or cocktails—she stops at a vending machine to pick up chips, chocolate, and soda this time.

"Uh, what are all those for?" I raise a suspicious brow at my sister, who's balancing everything in her arms.

Stacy smiles like I hadn't just confessed feeling guilty over Jasper's death. "I'm thinking junk-filled movie night. How about it? I know you have to wake up early, but one rom-com wouldn't hurt, right?"

If it weren't for that endearing smile, I'd say no. "Well, fine. It's not like I'll be getting much sleep anyway."

Stacy chuckles. "I know, right?"

With Rex trailing right behind us, we make our way to Stacy's suite. She clears her bed of clothes not yet hung and makes sure Rex and I are settled. She even has me slip into one of her silk sleepwear sets, and I admit—the soft fabric sliding over my skin feels nice.

Rex has his own corner, complete with his bed that Stacy thoughtfully took from my room.

"Thanks, Stace," I say, curling up next to her on the bed while the TV perches across the room on the wall.

Stacy barely glances at me as she scrolls through the movie options. "You'd do the same for me. Don't worry about it."

She settles on a classic rom-com: How to Lose a Guy in Ten Days. I ask, "Don't you want to talk about what happened tonight?"

Without warning, Stacy pops a potato chip into my mouth. "I love that you're more open about these things, Rosie-Posie, but tonight, I just want you to focus on the film, enjoy the junk food, fall asleep next to me, and wake up refreshed tomorrow... or with an upset stomach. Who knows?"

I laugh. "Alright, then. If you say so, sis."

The movie starts. We laugh, get giddy, even teary-eyed at some scenes. Sitting close together, passing chips and chocolates back and forth, I can't help but glance at Stacy, grateful for a sister who loves me like this.

At some point, Rex curls up by my feet, silently reminding me he's here.

Before the movie ends, my eyelids grow heavy. I let sleep pull me under. With Jasper's death looming, I don't know when I'll feel this calm again—like for once, my grim thoughts are tucked away.

By seven in the morning, my alarm blares. Stacy, usually a late sleeper, winces while I spring out of bed, fully refreshed from a rare good night's rest.

Health professionals may argue junk food before bed worsens insomnia, but I'd say it helped.

I toss off the duvet, set my feet on the floor. Rex yawns and hops down. Stacy groans. "You could be late, you know? I'm sure your boss wouldn't mind."

"I won't take that chance," I say, slipping off the silk sleepwear and into last night's clothes. I'll return to my room later for a shower and fresh outfit.

"See you later," I whisper to Stacy.

I'm ready for whatever Jasper's case throws at me, thanks to Stacy and Rex.

If Stacy weren't so sleepy, I bet she wouldn't let me go this easily. But she groans, rolling away, sunlight touching her face through the slightly drawn curtain. She clearly wants more sleep.

So, quietly, I dress, leash Rex, and slip out.

Walking from the deluxe suites onto a promenade deck, the morning sun peeks over the Atlantic horizon—stunning. Blues and greens ripple in the water, calming even someone who just found a dead body last night.

The air is cold, crisp, and fresh. Saltwater and brewed coffee scent the breeze, promising a good day.

Standing here, dwarfed by the vast ocean, my worries feel small in the grand scheme. Maybe this is what I needed—a moment of calm. A reminder that everything will be okay.

"It's a great morning, huh, bud?" I turn to Rex.

He barks happily, tongue lolling. I take that as a yes.

After a few minutes soaking up the sun and salty air, Rex and I head back to our designated room, nestled just above crew quarters and below some administrative offices.

Julia is pacing in the hallway, biting her nails, still in her poodle-themed pajamas.

As soon as she spots us, she rushes over. "Oh my gosh, Rose! Are you okay? I heard from Ben... I mean, Captain

Anderson, last night. What does he mean there's been a... murder on the ship?"

She lowers her voice on the M word.

I feel sorry Julia has to deal with this again. I'm glad she wasn't there last night to witness Jasper's strange death. But I won't lie to her.

"I'm sorry, Jules, but it's Jasper. It happened just after he left the casino."

Julia's face drains of color. "What? You mean after you talked to him?"

There it is—the moment I could've prevented his death. But I don't dwell. I'm accepting it's not my fault.

I shake my head. "I didn't get the chance. I had to help a guest who lost her son in the crowd. Then Mrs. Abernathy in the presidential suites called about a commotion, so I went to check. And it was Jasper. Dead when I got there."

Julia freezes, eyes widening. Then she pulls me in a hug. "I'm so sorry I wasn't there for you, Rose. I should've insisted on coming."

"Oh, come on." I pat her back. "I'm glad you didn't see it. But you can help with the investigation. What do you think?"

Julia pulls away, fear fading into resolve. "Absolutely! I'll get dressed, and we can start."

I nod, smiling sincerely. "Okay, I'll see you out here in half an hour?"

"Okay!" Julia runs back to her room, right across from mine.

Her enthusiasm makes me chuckle as I unlock my door.

Inside, the first thing I do is prepare Rex's food from a can. He happily digs in while I hop in the shower.

Soon after, I dress in a fresh black pantsuit with matching sneakers—practical for the long day of running around the ship ahead.

I tie my hair back in a ponytail, give Rex a quick once-over to make sure he's as adorable as ever, then meet Julia in the hall. Her lime green top over white pants nearly blinds me, and her earrings match perfectly.

"I'm ready." Julia pumps her fist in the air, and Rex spins happily between us.

I can't help but laugh.

Before I can reply, footsteps echo down the hallway. Ben, Stacy, and Cole appear.

"Perfect timing." Stacy smiles, dressed up for a day of cruising.

"I thought you were sleeping in." I smile at my sister, glad to see her nonetheless.

She shrugs. "I almost was. But as soon as you were out, I kept thinking you'd probably skip breakfast, and as your older sister, I can't let you start work on an empty stomach."

"I didn't think you were that thoughtful." I squint playfully.

Her smile breaks into a grin. "Well, I made a reservation at the restaurant. Fancy breakfast. My treat."

Ben chuckles. "I offered to pay with an employee discount, but your sister is stubborn. I see where you get that trait."

I gasp, feigning offense. "Excuse me? I am not stubborn. Stacy definitely is. Mine is debatable."

"Well, Stacy is stubborn," Cole mumbles, earning a playful nudge from Stacy.

"Hey!" she exclaims with a dramatic pout. "You're supposed to be on my side, Cole!"

After the hallway banter, we head to the restaurant on the upper decks, bathed once again in sunlight and the endless ocean view.

We sit around the table, enjoying breakfast orders—courtesy of Stacy.

In this moment, all is well. No one talks about murder. No one mentions my dissociation from last night.

Right now, we're just five people—and one dog—sharing a meal aboard The Midnight Tide.

I could've sworn the strawberries in my crepe tasted sweeter.

But I know the music I have to face is coming. Fifteen minutes after eight, my phone rings.

Already on duty, I check the caller ID: Dr. Bates.

I pick up. "Hello, Dr. Bates?"

The conversation about murder and death is back.

Chapter 8

Breakfast is cut short when duty calls. Luckily, I finished both my crepe and latte, so at least my stomach is full as we make our way down the narrow, cold, dim corridors leading to the morgue—which might be the worst thing right now.

My stomach twists thinking about Jasper's body laid out on a cold metal table—his torso cut open and stitched shut in three places.

I force the morbid images away.

Our footsteps echo sharply with each step—tap, tap, tap—like a ticking clock counting down. Even Rex picks up pace, matching the rhythm as we move forward. Ben and Cole follow behind me, while Stacy and Julia lag further back.

I don't want them to see the scene in the morgue. Not yet.

Down here, the ship feels alive in all the wrong ways—the metal hull groans and creaks; seawater splashes against it with a steady rhythm. Clanks and mechanical whirs break the silence, creating a harsh soundtrack that presses against my nerves.

Then, as we near the morgue, the distant sounds of Dr. Bates's portable Bluetooth speaker float through the hall—mellow seventies tunes drifting along with his quiet humming, as if his work doesn't revolve around dead bodies.

Unlike me. I'm sure he's used to this.

We step into the morgue.

Ben greets, "Good morning, Dr. Bates. Found anything interesting?"

"Well, hello there. If it isn't my favorite bunch." Dr. Bates swivels his chair to face us, a small smile tugging at his lips. "I have the conclusive result for Jasper Thorne's cause of death. Full report's still in progress."

Rex spins happily and places his front paws on Dr. Bates's knees. The doctor laughs and pats him on the head.

I keep my eyes off Jasper's body, covered by a white sheet on the metal table. I nod and ask, "What's the result, Doc?"

"Like I said last night—strangulation." Dr. Bates adjusts his glasses and continues. "Ligature strangulation, to be precise. The victim's neck shows unmistakable compression marks consistent with strong pressure applied by a cord-like object."

"A cord-like object?" I repeat.

He hands me a close-up photo of Jasper's neck. Despite my hesitation, I have to look. "As you can see, Miss Dela Cruz, the markings suggest a thin, flexible item was used. A shoelace would leave thinner marks, and a rope would show deeper impressions from knots. My guess? A fabric drawstring—probably from clothing. Most likely a hoodie."

The murder weapon sounds less gruesome than usual, but I can't stop a breathless gasp from slipping out. I quickly suppress it with a forced exhale.

A hoodie string? So innocent-looking. No—convenient. No one would suspect someone carrying a hoodie drawstring as a weapon. The killer could have simply walked into Jasper's suite with it, completely unnoticed.

Cole breaks in, "Any other findings, Doc?"

Dr. Bates nods. "Petechial hemorrhages in his face and eyes—typical with strangulation. No other significant trauma, just a slight bruise on his rib and a scratch on his hand—signs of struggle, but he didn't put up much of a fight."

Ben, Cole, and I exchange worried glances.

How terrible that Jasper tried to fight for his life...and still lost. He must have been caught off guard, coming back to celebrate his winnings only to be strangled in cold blood.

Dr. Bates clears his throat, "Oh, and one more thing." He reaches for the evidence box—where we keep items until we can hand them over at the next port.

Our attention shifts as he pulls out an evidence bag—the one with two gold poker chips placed over Jasper's eyes last night.

"These," Dr. Bates holds the bag up to the light, "were left over Jasper's eyes. Is that right?"

"Like a message," I murmur, unsure what it means.

"An odd message," Dr. Bates agrees with a sigh.

"Do you know what it means?" Cole asks, hope flickering in his voice.

When it comes to death, Dr. Bates is the expert, so I look to him as well.

His tone grows confident. "Have you heard of the ferryman?"

"You mean from Greek mythology?" Ben asks, brows furrowed.

"Exactly." Dr. Bates snaps his fingers and sets aside the evidence bag. "The ferryman transports the dead to the underworld but demands payment. That's why there's a tradition of placing coins over the eyes of the deceased—to pay the ferryman, so the dead don't wander the Earth."

For a moment, no one says a word. I let his words sink in: ferryman, payment, coins—only these are poker chips. But what does that mean for Jasper? Is someone paying respect? Or does the killer want to make sure Jasper crosses over?

"A penny for your thoughts, Miss Dela Cruz? Pun intended." Dr. Bates winks, watching my face as it shifts from confusion to contemplation.

I say, "It's just... it doesn't add up. Why would a cold-blooded killer, who strangled Jasper with a hoodie string, leave those chips as some kind of... respect? Like they want Jasper to cross over peacefully? It's counterintuitive."

"Or the guy's just a psychopath," Cole says flatly, scrunching his face. "Profiling shows killers who leave things behind are often... leaving signatures. Not clues exactly, but marks of power, control, or twisted artistry. Like the Zodiac Killer. They want to leave a mark."

"But the Zodiac was a serial killer," I whisper, a chill running down my spine. The last thing I want is a serial killer aboard this ship.

"You don't have to be a serial killer to want a signature," Cole shrugs, trying to ease the tension.

Dr. Bates nods. "Like you said, it's a message. Maybe not meant for us, but for someone else. The form is twisted, but if it's the killer's art, only he understands it."

"Yeah, but I think it's smarter not to leave any clues," I say, frustration biting at my words.

Despite the otherwise smart conversation, the killer's intentions feel more complicated. Or maybe the killer is complicated—a man, a woman, who knows? We barely know anything about this case.

Ben's hands settle on my shoulders with a firm, reassuring squeeze. "Let's just think about this: the clue's actually in our favor, right? It gives us a peek into the killer's personality—their twisted psyche."

I let my shoulders drop at Ben's touch. Between that and the hopeful look on Dr. Bates's face, I give in. "You're right. Maybe we need to look past the crime scene and get inside the killer's head."

Dr. Bates hands me the evidence bag with the gold poker chips. "That's a better look in your eyes, Miss Dela Cruz. Go on—get your investigation started. Maybe begin with those poker chips."

With a plan in place, we thank Dr. Bates and officially kick off the investigation. First order of business: figure out where the golden chips came from.

Cole excuses himself to contact authorities at our next port—Amber Cove, Puerto Plata. Meanwhile, Ben, Rex, and I head to the casino to find Jude.

Jude seems more relaxed than yesterday during the tournament—his hair slicked back, uniform crisp and crease-free. I almost feel bad for the questions we're about to throw at him, but he might know something about these gold chips.

"Mr. Romero!" Ben calls out, drawing Jude's attention with an easy smile. The casino's quiet this morning, few guests around. Maybe that's why Jude seems at ease, basking in the natural sunlight flooding the room.

Jude strides over, quick and purposeful. "Captain Anderson, Miss Dela Cruz. Didn't expect you this early. What brings you here?"

"Well, about last night's tournament..." I start. "There were cheating allegations. Did you look into them?"

Jude leans back, stretching his neck. "I spent all night reviewing the tournament footage, Miss Dela Cruz. Saw nothing out of place. I think the rumors about Jasper Thorne cheating just got players riled up."

Mental notes start forming. "Is that true? Does Jasper cheat?"

He shrugs reluctantly. "It's... a rumor. Even in this industry, gossip flies. Jasper's usually the target. Some say he's too good at poker for his own good, others say he's just lucky. But last night? No proof he cheated."

I nod slowly.

Before I respond, Jude continues, "Don't worry, I'll keep a closer eye on Mr. Thorne tonight."

My gaze shifts to Ben. His face remains unreadable as he delivers a half-truth. "Mr. Thorne won't be in the next tournament, Jude."

Jude's expression falls—confusion, then concern. "Is he alright? Did something happen?"

We don't want to stir panic on the ship. A killer is enough reason to worry, but it's better to keep control—no need to ruin anyone's vacation.

"He... was threatened last night," Ben says carefully. His clenched jaw betrays the lie, but Jude doesn't notice. "So Jasper's sitting out the tournament. Says it's not worth the risk."

"Was it a player who threatened him?" Jude lowers his voice, cautious.

"We're still investigating," I say, pulling out the evidence bag to reveal the gold poker chips. I shield the label carefully. "The attacker left this in Jasper's suite. Does this look familiar?"

Jude peers at the chips. "Familiar only because I've seen them elsewhere... but not here. We don't have gold chips."

"Just as I thought," I murmur, slipping the bag into my pocket. "Do you think it could be one of the players? Would you know who?"

"Only a few," Jude replies apologetically. "All I know is Jasper's got a bad reputation in the poker community. You saw his game last night—his luck's... unbelievable. No wonder players suspect cheating."

"But you said he's not cheating, right?"

"Last night? Ninety percent sure he didn't."

"Only ninety? What about the other ten?"

"When he was new, there were confirmed cheating incidents. Can't ignore that."

I glance at Ben, who's been listening intently. Finally, he speaks. "So, you confirm Jasper didn't cheat last night, and those gold chips aren't ours?"

"That's right, Captain." Jude nods firmly.

"Thanks, Jude," Ben says dismissively.

Without waiting, Jude nods and hurries away.

I can't help blurting out, "Can we trust him?"

Ben watches Jude disappear. "Rose, apart from us, who on this ship can we really trust?"

I turn to Rex, who stands quietly by my side. His gaze lingers on Jude's retreating figure. I can tell—he's just as unsure as I am.

Chapter 9

I step out of the casino with Ben, the arcade-like music still buzzing in my ears.

"I'm off to the bridge," he says.

Rex bumps his little head against Ben's leg in his usual goodbye, and I nod. "Of course. But what about Jasper's family? We have to call them today."

Ben briefly squeezes my hand, then lets go before anyone notices. "I'll take care of it, okay? You just focus on the investigation."

A flicker of hesitation hits me. I don't want to keep leaning on Ben for everything. But am I ready to carry this weight myself? I should be. I have to be. I meet his gaze and say, "I'll do it. I just need a moment to prepare myself for that conversation, but I'll do it."

"Rose, you don't have to—"

"I want to," I interrupt, forcing a smile. "You've been handling it for so long, but it should be me. It's my job to look after the passengers' welfare, isn't it?"

I have to say it now, before doubt creeps in and steals my courage. That heartbreaking call won't get easier, but I have to be the one to make it. I still have time today to steel myself.

Ben's eyes soften. Proud. Concerned but proud. "Are you sure about this?"

I nod. "Yes."

Even as passengers pass, Ben takes my hand again and squeezes it. "Fine. But I want to be there when you make the call, okay?"

"Okay," I say, this time the smile feeling real. Having Ben with me will help. For now, I let go. "I'll see you later. I'm going to find Cole."

We split up, each heading to our tasks. Rex and I walk to the security office at the far end of the lowest promenade deck. It's almost in the middle of the ship, between lower and upper decks—a spot easy for crew and passengers alike.

The cold air brushes my face, my dark hair whipping behind me as I walk into the wind. Rex doesn't mind; his little paws hop happily along our familiar path.

At the security office, a spacious room filled with tables and glowing computer screens, at least six men watch their monitors.

I knock twice before entering. The officers greet me warmly, and I return the gesture.

Cole's head pops out of his office the moment he hears my voice. "Rose, over here!"

Rex is already playing with one of the officers, who offers to watch him while I join Cole inside.

"Sorry to keep you waiting. We talked to the casino manager about the poker chips."

"No worries," Cole says, pulling a chair over to sit across from his computer. "I already pinpointed the exact time Jasper came back to his suite. Now, we just watch what happens next."

I take a deep breath, shifting closer to the screen. "Okay, I'm ready."

Cole presses a key, and the security footage flickers to life, showing Jasper walking into his suite, the black bag stuffed with money still in his hand.

"See?" I whisper. "He walked in with the bag, but it's gone from the room. Someone took it."

Cole nods, eyes glued to the screen. "We're about to find out who."

The flickering glow of the security feed casts an eerie light on our faces. Cole's office has no windows—just a long table, chairs, six huge screens on the wall, and two smaller ones on his desk.

We watch every movement outside Jasper's door, faces tight with focus and determination.

For five minutes, only a few passengers wander past on that floor.

My chest tightens. If I had pushed harder last night, maybe I'd have been there. But regret's useless now. I'll make it right by catching Jasper's killer. That's what matters.

Then, in the sixth minute, something shifts. Five men slip into frame, all wearing identical black hoodies with their hoods pulled low, faces hidden. The strings of their hoodies dangle like silent warnings.

A knot tightens in my stomach.

Cole pauses the video, zooms in, and grabs a screenshot. "Not every day we see five guys dressed exactly alike, heads down like that."

"Do you think it's... them?" My voice is barely a breath as I try to steady myself.

Cole's sigh carries the weight of doubt. "Deliberately evading cameras? They're definitely up to no good." He clicks play again.

The screen flickers. Four of the men scatter down the hallway. One pulls out a phone; another stops at the end of the hall, staring out at the dark ocean beyond. The rest wander aimlessly, heads bowed, faces hidden.

But the fifth guy keeps me tense. He stands still for a moment, then steps up and knocks on Jasper's door.

My heart drops.

Five seconds later, Jasper—unaware of the danger—opens the door. The man slips inside, shutting the door behind him.

If only we had cameras inside the suites...

I exhale sharply, fear rattling through me.

Cole and I sit frozen, watching. We can't rewind time or jump in to stop it. All we can do is wait for the killer to appear again.

Cole tries turning up the volume, but we only hear static, creaking boards, the ocean, and faint murmurs. Useless.

Then Mrs. Abernathy, Jasper's next-door neighbor, peeks out of her room. She doesn't seem to notice the hooded men. Maybe to her, they're just passengers in dark clothes.

She glances around, then retreats into her room.

This is the moment she calls me.

Again, the thought that I might have saved Jasper swirls in my mind.

I push it down. I have to talk to her after this.

Another minute ticks by. Just three minutes before Jasper's door finally opens. The hooded man pulls his hood tighter, shadowing his face as he slips away from the scene. At the same time, the other four men start moving.

Cole freezes the screen, zooming in on the black bag now clutched in the man's hand.

"So, that's where it went," Cole mutters, his face twisting into a grim scowl. I can see he wishes we could do more than just watch.

My eyes fix on the paused frame. The hoodie strings of the guy who entered Jasper's room are gone now. He's hidden the murder weapon.

Cole grabs another screenshot and hits play again. The men rush down the hall, still dodging the cameras, walking close together.

Cole skillfully tracks them through multiple cameras—until they reach the staircase near the reception, where emergency stairs and two hallways meet.

A blind spot.

Suddenly, the man with the money bag vanishes.

The other four split up, scattering down different corridors, deliberately confusing us.

I realize—they knew we'd be watching.

Their plan was elaborate, calculated.

If I'm honest, they did an impressive job avoiding the cameras, all dressed alike so distinguishing them was impossible.

Four accomplices. One killer. Five hundred passengers aboard The Midnight Tide.

Dread crawls from my stomach into my chest, squeezing tight. My heart feels like it's suffocating under the weight. But I don't give in. Not now.

Silence falls between Cole and me. Then a soft whimper breaks it—Rex, curled under my chair, joining our moment of despair.

"Oh, hey there," I say, managing a smile as I scratch behind his ear.

Cole finally breaks the quiet. "What now? I'm pretty sure we can't ID them from the footage. They knew every blind spot."

"We still have to try," I say, voice steady as if my resolve hadn't wavered. "I'll have Julia spend hours combing through this, tracking each hooded figure. One of them will slip up."

Murder scheme... the words catch in my throat.

Cole nods. "I'll get my men watching the same. It'd be impossible to check every passenger with a matching build. Finding those jackets alone would take forever."

"I know," I admit, bitterness twisting my gut. If I could, I'd search every closet on this ship for suspects. But there are better ways.

"Instead of chasing looks, we need to focus on motive," I suggest.

"Didn't you say Jasper pissed off a lot of people?" Cole asks.

"That's true. But not everyone's reason is strong enough for murder."

Cole frowns, thinking. "I heard he won $250,000. That's a tempting reason."

I sigh. "It does sound tempting."

He brightens with an idea. "If that's the case, wouldn't the people who knew about his winnings be the same ones who attended the tournament?"

I consider that. "True, but we live-streamed the entire event. Anyone with a phone or computer on this ship could've seen Jasper win."

"So what if the real target wasn't Jasper—but the tournament winner?" Cole suggests.

I hesitate. My mind races, gears turning fast.

I reply, "Jasper's luck is famous in the poker world. My theory? The killer knew he'd win and used that as cover—making it look like a robbery gone wrong. But the real motive shows in the $2,000 worth of gold poker chips left behind—a twisted send-off to Jasper's afterlife."

Cole can't help but grin. "There it is, Rose! 'Look into the mind of the killer,' Dr. Bates said. You're doing it."

Despite the sinking feeling, I chuckle. "We'd better keep thinking. This killer could get away if we don't."

"We won't let that happen." Cole's confidence is contagious. "We've cracked cases like this before. When have we ever let a murderer slip through?"

Rex barks in agreement.

This time, I laugh.

Cole's right. We won't let this cruise end without handing a killer over to the police.

The killer might be smart... but that means only one thing: we have to be smarter.

Chapter 10

The dining hall bustles with a motley crowd from all decks of The Midnight Tide—nimble servers weaving through hungry guests, bleary-eyed high rollers nursing their first but definitely not last coffee, and the last few not-so-early birds grabbing what's left of breakfast.

On a ship this size, tracking down the right people to talk to about Jasper feels like searching for a needle in a haystack. But then I spot them—the same men who played in the tournament last night, all clustered around one table.

"That's them, right? The guys we're interviewing first?" Cole's voice is low, barely cutting through the hum of chatter and clinking silverware.

Without a suspect list, the closest we've got are these guys—none of whom were particularly close to Jasper. Ironic.

How I wish Jasper had come with a plus-one. Maybe then we'd have a place to start instead of hoping a bunch of men who clearly hated his guts might have something useful to say.

Still, I tell Cole, "They're in the same industry as Jasper. Maybe they know something."

More a reassurance for myself than a reply to him.

Cole nods and strides past the sprawling buffet—pastries, omelets, cereals, fruit, yogurt—toward the high rollers' table. Clearing his throat, he calls out, "Excuse me, sirs..."

The low murmur quiets as they turn toward Cole and me. Rex pads along at my side, stopping just beside us.

Seven out of the ten players from last night gathered here for breakfast tells me this poker tournament is all friendly fun—except when it comes to Jasper.

I glance around the table—no empty chairs waiting for anyone... especially not Jasper.

"Can we help you?" The man closest to Cole asks.

Cole glances at me, urging me to start, so I do. "Is this a good time to ask you some questions?"

"About what?" another voice cuts in.

"About..." I hesitate a fraction, careful not to sound suspicious. "...Jasper Thorne. He was threatened last night, so we're looking into it."

I go with the same line Ben gave Jude earlier. Threatened sounds a hell of a lot better than murdered.

The group exchanges skeptical glances—none buying it. One smirks, sipping his coffee to hide it. Another shakes his head, amusement flickering across his face. Someone even snickers—stopping only because we're watching.

Then the businessman—Anthony Dickins, I now know—shrugs. "I don't know why you're asking us. We're not fond of the guy—couldn't care less about him."

The smug look on Anthony's face as he casually scoops crème brûlée from his ramekin irritates me. I push forward. "I believe you were bothered by Mr. Thorne last night."

"Who wouldn't be?" Anthony replies, licking sugary residue from his lips. "The guy cheats during the tournament. I stopped buying the 'just luck' excuse a while ago. No one's that lucky. Honestly, I'm glad someone threatened him; it's about time someone called him out."

"Any idea who might've done that?" I press, tilting my head to show interest.

Anthony holds my gaze only briefly before scanning the table instead. "Anyone want to confess? Come on, we won't judge. Hell, I might even buy the winner the priciest bottle on this ship."

Laughter bubbles around the table.

"No takers?" Anthony asks, dripping sarcasm. Then he faces me again. "Sorry, miss. Looks like the culprit isn't here."

Their borderline disrespect triggers Cole, who steps in with a voice deeper and firmer than usual—meant to intimidate. "Let me try again. Can anyone here tell us about the threat Mr. Thorne received last night? You're in the same circle, even if you won't share his table. You can keep joking—or I can take you to one of our offices and hold you there for hours until someone talks. And yes, I say that as head of security on The Midnight Tide."

A hush falls, like the entire dining hall dropped the volume a few notches. But it's really just this table stifling their laughter.

Clearing his throat, Anthony shifts to a more serious tone. "Anyone want to speak up?"

For a beat, silence reigns. Instead, they do little things to shake off the tension—sip coffee, check watches, glance down the buffet line, slice cold steak and eggs.

Finally, the hedge fund manager—Andy Chen—breaks it. "I don't know if it's related to last night, but Jasper has a ton of enemies. It's no secret he owes a lot of people money. For someone who lucks out at poker this much, he's deep in debt."

Cole and I exchange curious looks. Even Rex stares up at me, eyes wide.

How's that possible? I wonder.

If Jasper suspiciously wins most of his games, how can he still be drowning in debt? Last night alone, he took home a quarter of a million dollars.

Bad spending? Or a mountain of debt too big to clear, no matter how lucky he is? If only I could ask him myself.

The group murmurs agreement at Andy's words. One pipes up, "I heard he owed that businessman—the oil rig guy."

Another adds, "Oil rig? I thought he owed that real estate tycoon lady hundreds of thousands."

Cole and I digest the info as it flows out naturally now.

"The one from California?"

"Yeah, that's the one."

"Didn't he also owe a councilor in L.A.?"

"At this point, he owes everybody we know."

No laughter, just snickers and nods. Like it's all painfully true.

I file away every detail in my mental notes.

Cole tries his luck. "Out of those—the oil rig guy, the real estate lady, and the councilor—is any of them on the ship? Or someone connected to them? Anyone know?"

That's Cole rolling the dice. What are the chances the name of someone Jasper owes money to also happens to be on The Midnight Tide?

The table of high rollers pauses mid-conversation, considering. I almost cross my fingers—tiny hope sparking that luck might finally turn our way. It doesn't always have to be Jasper's luck.

Then Andy snaps his fingers like he's just remembered something. "Ah! That trust fund kid! I thought I saw him last night at the casino."

"Trust fund kid?" My eyes widen with a flicker of excitement. Could this be our first real lead?

"Yeah, what's his name again...?" Andy asks his friends, each pausing to think.

Come on, I urge silently. Please don't let me miss out on a name to pin on our whiteboard. Any name, any clue—anything.

After watching the security footage and coming up empty, there has to be something these men can tell us.

Finally, someone speaks up. "Oh! Benson Wolf! That's it."

I feel my chest rise, a sigh slipping free.

"So, Benson Wolf... Jasper owes him money too? Right?" I confirm.

"Oh, yeah," Andy replies. "That Wolf kid practically throws money at anyone who asks. But last I heard, Jasper stopped paying Benson what he owed—and Benson wasn't happy about it."

Loan shark vibes? Is Benson Wolf some kind of dangerous debtor like those I see on TV?

A chill creeps up my arms, making my skin prickle. "So, what did Benson do?"

Andy shrugs—either unsure or indifferent. "Who knows? You should ask Jasper yourself. Maybe tell him to stop pissing people off."

I nod, even though I can't tell Jasper that—not when he's locked inside one of those morgue cabinets in the lower decks.

"Well, thanks for the tip," I say, preparing to leave.

"Excuse us," Cole adds as we slowly back away from the table.

Before we're even out of earshot, Anthony mutters, "Serves him right..."

I ignore the jab and pull my phone from my pocket. I dial Julia. She picks up on the third ring. "Rose! Need something?"

"Yes. Search the passenger database for Benson Wolf. Get me everything you can."

No questions—just tapping sounds from her side. She's already on it. "Okay... Benson Wolf... hmm—oh! He's in room A22."

Same floor as Jasper—but on the opposite side, I note.

"Anything interesting on him?" I ask, knowing a cruise database usually just holds basics and emergency contacts. But these days, we sometimes check criminal histories, just in case. Maybe Julia will find something.

More clacking. "Hmm... nothing noteworthy. A quick search shows he owns a gaming company. His dad was a big exec at some huge tech firm."

Loan shark? The thought lingers, but even in my head, it feels judgmental. I shouldn't assume without meeting him.

Instead, I ask, "Any scandals? News stories? Gossip?"

Julia murmurs, distracted. "Nope. Nothing."

"That's fine," I say with a small smile. "While you're at it, send his photo to security. We want to find him fast."

"Got it!"

"Thanks, Jules." I end the call and turn to Cole. "Let's go find Benson Wolf."

Chapter 11

I flinch at the sight of the empty poker tournament table where Jasper spent his last hour alive.

Still, Cole and I stand at the entrance to the vibrant casino, scanning the crowd of serious gamblers and casual players for Benson.

"Hey." Ben creeps up behind us. "I heard on the radio you were making your way here. Figured I'd join you. But first—who's Benson Wolf?"

Ben may be the captain, but he's never too busy to know everything happening on his ship.

I crane my neck, searching for Benson. "Uh, he's someone Jasper owes money to."

Ben raises his eyebrows in surprise. "And he happens to be on the ship?"

"Yeah. I know." I shrug. "Coincidence or not?"

Ben lowers his voice as a couple steps out of the casino. "I don't believe in coincidences—not with murder. So, where is he?"

"That guy over there." Julia's voice cuts through the noise, pulling me around. Her mild, flowery perfume drifts through the air. "Sorry, I just had to come over. I want to help."

Rex immediately wags his tail and stands on his hind legs to greet her. Julia doesn't hesitate; she takes Rex's leash from me and pets him.

I smile. "Glad you came—I haven't spotted him yet."

Julia points to a man half-hidden behind a slot machine. "That blond guy with the wavy hair? That's him. I've been staring at his photo for half an hour, so I know."

I follow her finger, then glance back at the group. "We don't want to intimidate Benson Wolf with all four of us, right?"

Cole quickly suggests, "You and Captain Anderson should talk to him. I'll keep watch."

"And I'll... go find Jude," Julia chimes in, lifting Rex's leash to show he's coming with me.

Ben and I make our way to Benson, our footsteps muffled by the thick carpet. Even without it, the clatter from the games and music from the speakers drown out everything else.

A few strides bring us to the slot machines, where a surprisingly young guy—early thirties maybe—sits casually, blue light reflecting off his face.

Though I saw his photo earlier, he looks younger in person. Maybe it's the clean-shaven face—different from the circulated picture.

He doesn't look like a dangerous debtor. More like one of those skateboard kids you see in magazines promoting street style.

Could he be one of those five hooded men? No way. But murderers don't have a type—just a shared thirst for blood.

Ben nudges me, lips moving silently, "You okay?"

I blink back to reality, nodding at him, then call out to the man at the slot machine. "Mr. Wolf?"

Benson lazily turns away from the spinning screen, bored. "Yeah?"

"I'm Rose Dela Cruz, cruise director of The Midnight Tide. This is Captain Ben Anderson."

"Captain?" Benson spins his chair to face us, frowning. "If you're here, who's driving the ship?"

He laughs at his own joke before we can respond. "That was lame, huh? I don't get to meet captains every day. Anyway, what can I do for you?"

So laid-back and funny. Got it.

I clear my throat, diving into the explanation we've repeated so many times. "We want to ask about Jasper Thorne. Last night, he was threatened. We understand you and Jasper have… a complicated relationship."

Benson makes a sizzling noise with his mouth, unconcerned. "And Jasper said I threatened him?"

"Well, not exactly Jasper…" I mumble, knowing he couldn't name anyone even if he wanted to.

Benson crosses his arms. "It'd be pretty shameless of him to say I made him uncomfortable. I'm a courteous guy. I even let him be last night."

"What's that supposed to mean?" The slot machine screen behind Benson suddenly goes black, and my head spins with questions.

He studies my face, gauging how much I know. "That complicated relationship? It's about money—my money. Jasper owes me. Hasn't paid in months."

His words come in short bursts for emphasis. "The guy's been avoiding me, so when I heard he was in the poker tournament on this cruise, I booked the same trip. You know? To remind him he still owes."

Everything about Benson screams ease—a man confident in his words or completely unbothered.

No murder weapon hidden in his luggage, like a drawstring from a hoodie.

But that confidence sets off an itch I can't scratch. Where is it coming from? How can he casually talk about Jasper's debts like it's small talk?

Ben cuts in. "By 'remind,' do you mean... scare him into paying?"

"Oh, dear lord, no." Benson chuckles, amused. "I don't think Jasper even knows I'm here. Sure, I watched the tournament last night—I was around. But I figured, since he's here, he should at least get a night to enjoy the cruise... and his winnings, right?"

Something in his words feels ominous, making my skin crawl. But I keep the questions sharp. "So, you didn't approach Jasper last night? Not even visit his suite?"

"I don't even know where his suite is." Benson shrugs. "But if you tell me, I'll pay him a visit now."

A visit? To Jasper's empty, crime-scene suite? Does Benson really not know Jasper's dead? Or is he messing with us?

My eyebrows knit. "So it wasn't you?"

"Who threatened Jasper?" Benson shoots back. "No. But I might threaten him soon if he keeps dodging me. So, suite number? Anyone?"

Ben and I exchange baffled looks. Benson's easy charm has downplayed the gravity of stalking Jasper on a cruise ship.

As I process everything, Ben replies to Benson's odd request. "I'm not sure I'm comfortable giving out Mr. Thorne's suite number... not after you just said you 'might' threaten him, too. Your words, Mr. Wolf."

Benson doesn't flinch. He just raises his arms like he's surrendering. "Understood, Captain. Glad to know this ship's run by reliable people. Now, can I get back to my game?"

Ben glances at me for confirmation. I nod and say, "Thank you for your time, Mr. Wolf."

Benson swivels back to the slot machines, and Ben and I step aside, walking away.

Once out of earshot, I say, "I don't think he knows what happened to Jasper."

Ben doesn't cave. "Or he's just a damn good liar."

"There's no argument there," I admit. We're still far from figuring out who killed Jasper Thorne.

This game's just beginning—one where poker faces and bluffs can be mistaken for truth.

I suggest, "We should keep an eye on Benson. Just in case."

"Agreed," Ben says.

We head back toward the entrance, where Cole talks quietly with Stacy. But before we close the gap, Rex suddenly barks from across the casino—uncharacteristic for him.

Guests glance our way as Ben and I hurry to Julia, crouched on the floor, cooing, "Hey, buddy. What's wrong?"

Rex ignores Julia, growling at something.

"What is it, Rex?" I ask as I reach them.

Julia stands and looks up at me. "I'm not sure what he's trying to say—he just started growling and barking."

I crouch too. "Hey, bud. What is it?"

Rex whimpers, then turns his gaze back to whatever has caught his attention.

Following his eyes, I realize he's not watching something. It's someone.

The woman from last night—the one glaring at Jasper during the tournament.

Blonde hair, red lipstick, a beauty mark above her upper lip. She wears a sleeveless linen wrap dress with a plunging neckline—casual casino chic.

Sunlight streams behind her through the huge windows, casting a halo that almost mimics the blue ocean outside.

Her eyes scan the cavernous room, searching for someone.

Rex looks up at me again, whimpering, urging me forward.

I've been curious about her since last night. Seeing her here is my chance to talk.

There has to be a reason she glared at Jasper like that.

Trusting Rex's instincts, I inhale and approach her. "Excuse me, miss?"

She turns, annoyance immediately crossing her face. "Yes?"

I should have prepared what to say, but instead, I just ask. "Do you know Mr. Jasper Thorne?"

Her expression shifts from irritation to mild surprise. "Who's asking?"

"Oh, I'm Rose Dela Cruz," I say softly, offering a smile. "Cruise director. And you are?"

She sighs, suppressing it. "Ida Birch. And why are you asking about Jasper?"

"I've noticed you last night." I'm straightforward. "You were watching the poker tournament. You seemed interested in Mr. Thorne."

Ida's eyes widen, caught red-handed. Her cheeks flush slightly. "I—I'm not interested in Jasper, alright? I just…

recognized him. Didn't think it was the cruise director's business."

"Oh, of course not." I chuckle lightly. "It's just that Mr. Thorne's concerned about his... safety. Something happened last night, and—"

"Is he okay?" Ida cuts in, pupils dilating with genuine worry.

I press on, "How do you know Mr. Thorne?"

Her face tightens; she clears her throat, as if something's stuck. "I'm... someone he used to know. Let's leave it at that."

"An ex-girlfriend?" I guess.

Ida blushes, stammering. "No! We went out a few times. It didn't work out. That's it."

A lover scorned—that thought flashes through me as her embarrassment morphs into a scowl.

Suddenly, she snaps, "I don't know why you're asking this. It feels inappropriate."

"I'm sorry if I made you uncomfortable," I say quickly. But I keep fishing for answers. "I'm looking into who could've bothered Mr. Thorne last night. Seeing how upset you are, I think it's safe to say you and Jasper didn't part well?"

Ida scoffs, flipping her hair back. "So? I don't like the guy. Boohoo. That's not a crime. And whatever you're implying, I want no part of Jasper. So please, leave me alone."

I'm tempted to ask if she's waiting for Jasper—she glances often toward the entrance and poker tables—but she's too annoyed, so I step back. "Alright, Miss Birch. Sorry to spring this on you."

She eyes me head to toe, then turns sharply and walks away before I can respond.

Julia and Rex rush to my side. "Oh my gosh, that was intense," Julia says. "I'm right, aren't I? Lover scorned?"

"I thought the same," I admit, watching Ida wander the casino.

"Think she could've done something to Jasper?" Julia asks, curiosity sharpening her tone—her job now involves solving murders.

I shake my head slowly. "I don't know yet. But I have a feeling we haven't seen the last of her."

"Then it's settled." Julia nods firmly. "I'm keeping a close watch on Ida Birch."

Chapter 12

As we pull away from the casino and pass one of the promenade decks, The Midnight Tide rocks gently beneath the sun. The endless blue ocean stretches past the metal guardrails, shimmering and teasing with every ripple.

Ben, Cole, and Julia return to their stations, slipping back into the rhythm of the ship's daily grind. Meanwhile, I'm left to piece together our next move in this relentless investigation.

Stacy and Rex stay close, brainstorming with me.

The salty breeze brushes my face, and for a fleeting second, I let myself pretend this is just a quiet, sunlit moment. But honestly? Serenity feels impossible in the middle of a murder case.

Especially when my phone suddenly rings—and the caller ID flashes Morgue (Dr. Bates).

I freeze. "Hello, Dr. Bates?"

Turning away from the wind so I can catch every word, I watch Stacy pause, Rex at her side, sensing something's up.

"Oh, Miss Dela Cruz, I hope I'm not catching you at a bad time," Dr. Bates says, his voice echoing through the empty morgue—the only sounds the quiet hum of the ship and two bodies, one tucked away in a cold cabinet.

"Not at all, Doctor. I'm just wandering the ship. What's going on?"

"I hope you can help. Listen," he sighs, and then a muffled ringing cuts through the line. "It's the phone. Can you hear it ringing?"

Against the backdrop of the ship's thrumming and wind, I faintly catch the sound. "Yes, I hear it. What about it?"

"It's coming from the evidence box you left here," Dr. Bates explains. "It's been ringing nonstop for the last fifteen minutes. I don't want to mess up your investigation by digging through Jasper's things. Can you check it out?"

A chill shoots down my spine.

Jasper's phone ringing isn't strange in itself—his friends or family could be trying to reach him after his sudden silence last night. But something about this call unsettles me.

After a pause, I say, "I'm on my way."

The call ends.

I turn to Stacy with fresh determination. "I have to go to the morgue. Can you—"

"I'm coming with you," Stacy cuts in firmly.

I was about to suggest she stay behind, but her steady gaze stops me. I could say no, but I don't want to.

The hallway to the morgue is always colder, quieter than anywhere else on the ship. Having company won't hurt.

Besides, with Jasper's body hidden away, I'd rather spare Stacy the harsh sight on Dr. Bates's work table.

Still, I ask, "You sure? It's the morgue."

Stacy shrugs, eyebrows raised. "Yeah. So?"

"Okay... if you say so." I lead the way into the maze of employee-only staircases and dim hallways weaving through the ship's lower decks.

No guests wander here, so the lights are low, walls bare except for portholes spilling specks of sunlight. The floors gleam faintly, marked only by a few lone footprints—ghostly in the flickering light.

Stacy and Rex trail behind me. She scans the space, searching for something—anything—beyond exposed pipes and endless corridors.

The ringing grows louder as we near the morgue.

It's been ten minutes since Dr. Bates called—meaning the phone has been ringing for twenty-five straight.

I pick up my pace, jogging the last stretch. Dr. Bates paces nervously in the center of the room. The evidence box we left is on the metal table. Jasper's phone, sealed in a clear plastic bag, sits next to it.

"Good, you're here," Dr. Bates says, relieved. "I don't know what to do about this. It just keeps ringing."

And it really does.

I approach cautiously, each step deliberate, like I'm defusing a bomb.

Standing over the phone, I glance at the screen. The caller ID says Boss.

Boss?

I blink. Jasper's an independent gambler. Why would he have a boss? Does he have a job I don't know about?

Dr. Bates hands me a yellow Post-It. "I wrote down the number in case you need it."

I slip it into my pocket.

Rex nudges my leg, urging me forward.

Taking the hint, I lift the phone from the bag, warmth against my palm. I hesitate, then press the green button, holding the phone to my ear.

"Thank God you picked up! I almost thought you were avoiding me. Now, tell me—where are you? We should meet, don't you think?" The man's voice is breathy, like he's been holding his breath for this moment.

I don't say a word. I just listen.

"Hello...? Come on, man. Stop jerking around. Where's the money from last night, huh?"

My breath catches, but I keep it steady. A flood of questions rushes through my mind—Who is this? Why does he care about Jasper's money?

The man curses under his breath, then hangs up.

The disconnected tone rings in my ear even as I set the phone down.

Dr. Bates watches me expectantly. "So? What's going on?"

"I—I'm not sure," I admit. "More questions than answers. But I need to let Ben and Cole know. I'll keep this phone with me for now, okay?"

Without waiting for a reply, I head for the door.

"Good luck, Miss Dela Cruz," Dr. Bates calls after me.

Stacy, Rex, and I hurry out of the morgue the same way we came in. I tuck Jasper's phone deep inside my coat pocket, its weight suddenly heavier than before.

"What was that about?" Stacy asks, falling a step behind me.

"I don't know. But it feels off," I admit, glancing back at her. "Can you call Cole? Tell him to meet us at the bridge?"

"I'm coming too?" Stacy asks, already dialing.

"Well, I thought you wanted to come," I say with a small smile. As much as I like having Stacy around, my mind is spinning from that strange phone call.

Behind me, Stacy tells Cole to head straight to the bridge.

We walk in silence through the cold hallways and echoing staircases, on a mission to get to the heart of the ship and figure this out together.

At the bridge, officers and crew barely glance up as they monitor radar screens, charts, and communication systems. The 180-degree windows flood the room with sunlight and an endless ocean view.

I've always admired this room—this is where our floating city stays afloat. But right now, my thoughts fixate on one thing: Jasper's phone.

I spot Ben and Cole near the small conference table and don't waste time. I set the phone down. "This is Jasper's phone. I just answered a call from someone he saved as 'Boss.'"

Ben turns to me, surprised. "Boss? Jasper's working for someone else?"

"He shouldn't be," I say. "Jasper's always been an independent gambler. He even came on board alone. But now... I don't think he was."

"What makes you say that?" Cole asks, frowning.

I look between them, explaining, "The caller said they should meet and asked about money from last night. If I'm right, Jasper came with someone—maybe even owes them money."

Ben's face tightens, then relaxes. "Show me the number. Let's run it through the passenger database."

Luckily, Dr. Bates already wrote it down.

I pull out the yellow Post-It and hand it over. Ben grabs his laptop and starts typing. Cole, Stacy, Rex, and I crowd around, waiting.

No match.

"Of course," I mutter. Nothing's ever easy when people don't want to be found—or caught.

Ben pulls out his phone. "I'll try calling."

He dials and puts it on speaker. Silence fills the room, then the robotic message: "The person you are trying to reach is currently unavailable."

I exhale. "Safe to say he turned off his phone?"

"Or worse, maybe he dropped the number," Cole says, grim.

Stacy, quiet until now, looks up. "I just Googled it. Jasper's biography says he's a prominent poker player. No job records. What if 'Boss' is code? Like part of a... mafia or something?"

Cole grins at Stacy's theory.

I shake my head, smiling too. "That's a stretch. The guy didn't sound mafia-ish. If anything, friendly... at first."

"So, who the heck is this boss?" Cole wonders aloud.

"Maybe someone who knows Jasper can tell us," Ben says, glancing my way, concern clear.

I know what he means—it's time to call Jasper's family.

Clenching my fists, I nod. "No point in waiting. They deserve the truth. We need answers."

Chapter 13

I can do this, I tell myself, staring at Jasper's phone in my hand. The person who knows him best must be the one on his speed dial. Officially, his emergency contact is his mother in the passenger database—but I doubt she knows all his secrets.

We all agree on that.

If Jasper's up to something shady, the last person who'd know is his mom.

So here I am, holding Jasper's phone like it's a ticking bomb, as if testing its weight is somehow going to prepare me for what's next.

"It's okay, Rose." Stacy's hand presses gently to the small of my back. Comfort. Reassurance. "We're here for you."

I've heard it a hundred times from this same circle of friends. But it still soothes me now, especially with my heart pounding so loud I can barely hear my own thoughts.

How did Ben do this before? How did he stay steady? Because I don't think I can.

But I have to.

Four pairs of eyes watch me—Stacy, Ben, Julia, and even Rex. I swallow down the lump in my throat and finally press Jasper's speed dial.

A name pops up on the screen: Jasmine.

Maybe a girlfriend? The name suggests so.

I move the phone to my ear, wishing for a little privacy in this moment. For now.

After all, I have no clue how the person on the other end will take the news that Jasper was murdered last night.

I dread it already.

Ring. Ring. Ring...

This time, the call connects. My chest rises and falls with uneven breaths, like I'm gasping for air underwater.

Then, click.

"Hey, Jasper! What's up?" Jasmine's voice is playful, unaware—blissfully oblivious—to the crushing news I'm about to deliver. I feel an instant stab of sympathy for her, the poor girl who gets the call first, only to face the questions after.

"Hi. Jasmine, right?" I force the words out before my voice breaks.

"Oh." Her tone drops, taking a serious turn. "Hi. Who is this? Why are you calling from Jasper's phone?"

"Hi . . ." I repeat, throat tightening. "I'm Rose Dela Cruz, cruise director of The Midnight Tide. You're on Jasper's speed dial, so we're calling you instead. Can I ask how you're related to him?"

On the surface, I'm holding it together. Inside, every word tastes bitter and heavy.

I focus on Jasmine's voice, blocking out the hum and beeps of the ship's navigation systems buzzing faintly in the background.

"I'm his sister—well, twin sister. Jasper and I are fraternal twins," Jasmine says, offering just enough to stall, like she senses something's wrong but isn't ready yet. Then she asks quietly, "Should I be worried?"

Worried doesn't even come close.

Grief isn't just worry. It's a bottomless ache, a twisting pain no word can fully capture.

I've seen people try to name grief, but it always slips through.

I glance at Ben, needing his silent strength. Jasmine doesn't need synonyms for worried; she needs the truth.

Without hesitation, Ben reaches out and tangles his fingers with mine.

I take a shaky breath. "I'm so sorry to call you like this, Jasmine. But something happened to your brother last night."

Pause.

We both need it.

When she doesn't speak, I push on.

"There's no easy way to say this, but . . . your brother was murdered last night."

Silence. Complete and suffocating.

"Jasmine?" My voice cracks. No answer—only soft, heartbreaking sobs.

She cries. Quietly at first, then louder, her grief spilling out in gasps and heaves, muffled screams caught in between.

I stand there, clutching Ben's hand like a lifeline in this bitter reality.

I bite my lower lip, fighting back my own tears as I listen to her heartbreak.

She cries for what feels like forever.

Finally, when she pulls herself together enough to breathe, her voice trembles, "What happened to him?"

I swallow the lump threatening to burst free. "He was strangled. We think it was a robbery gone wrong—he won a quarter million at last night's poker tournament. His winnings were missing, too."

Jasmine whimpers, struggling to hold herself upright. "And who did it? Have they caught the person?"

I wish I had better news. "No, not yet. The killer managed to avoid every security camera. And there were accomplices, which makes it harder to pin this on one person."

"Oh my gosh," Jasmine says, voice cracking. "What am I supposed to tell Mom? What do I do now?"

Her questions sound like cries to the heavens, not just to me.

I don't have answers. Instead, I say, "Look, Jasmine, I know there's nothing I can say to ease this pain. But we're going to do everything we can to find who did this, okay?"

She sniffs, voice small but fierce. "You have to. Jasper—he wasn't perfect. Far from it. But he didn't deserve this. What happened to him? It's awful. I—I don't know what to do now. What should I do?"

"We'll figure it out, Jasmine." My chest tightens as I keep talking. "How about we fly you out to our next port of call? All expenses paid—flight, hotel, everything. We'll be in Amber Cove tomorrow. We'll also arrange for Jasper's body to be transported. You can meet us there. How does that sound?"

"I can't think!" I imagine Jasmine pulling at her hair in frustration as we talk. This has to be the hardest conversation she's ever had with a stranger on the phone.

After a moment, she steadies herself.

"You know what? I'll do it. I want to be there when Jasper . . ." Her voice breaks, choking on tears. ". . . gets there. I'm sure he'd want to see his sister first, right?"

I don't know Jasper or Jasmine personally, but hearing Jasmine's voice crack on every syllable tells me one thing—she loves Jasper deeply. And the fact that she's on his speed dial? That's sibling love, plain and simple. How could it not be? They had nine more months than the rest of us to get to know each other—in the womb.

So I tell Jasmine, "I think that's exactly what Jasper wants."

Though I can't see her, I feel her nodding—convincing herself more than anyone else. "Thank you."

Before I can say anything else—comfort her, offer my condolences—the line goes dead. Jasmine's ended the call.

I keep the phone pressed to my ear for a few more seconds, as if it's the only thing holding me upright. When I finally set it down, my knees buckle like I'm made of paper.

Ben and Stacy catch me fast, gripping my arms.

"Are you okay?" Ben asks, leading me toward a nearby chair and pulling it out like a true gentleman. Then he heads to the pantry, grabs a bottle of water, opens it, and hands it to me.

I take the bottle, feeling the cool moisture in my hand—but I don't drink.

Stacy pulls another chair close. "Hey, good job, Rosie-Posie. You did great."

Despite her smile, I shake my head. "Did I? All I did was make Jasper's sister cry."

"Well, what did you expect?" Stacy teases, a hint of sarcasm in her voice.

I let out an empty chuckle and turn to Ben, who's standing over me, concern etched on his face. "How did you do it before? I felt like I was going to throw up the whole time I was talking to Jasmine."

"That means you're doing it right," Ben says, squeezing my shoulder gently. "Now, do you want a moment? You can rest for a few hours if you need."

That's just Ben—always taking care of me whenever he can. Headache? Sit down. Hangover? Here's your cure. Bad day? Got your favorite cake or ice cream. Just told Jasper's sister her twin brother is dead? Take a few hours.

In Ben's world, there's always a way to look after me—even when he's my boss and we're on duty.

I appreciate the offer, but I shake my head. There's too much left to do. "I've got to get Jasmine on a plane and settled in a nice hotel today. It's the least I can do for her."

"So, we'll see her tomorrow?" Cole's voice is low, almost like he's afraid it'll break me.

"After we turn over Jasper's body to the authorities and get everything settled," I say firmly.

Ben nods, knowing work is the best distraction I have right now. He turns to Cole. "You've contacted the authorities, right?"

"I made the call this morning. They'll be waiting for us at the port tomorrow," Cole replies.

"Good," Ben says, still with his hand on my shoulder. "That leaves us the rest of the day to dig for more information—clues about Jasper's death."

"I wouldn't want to spend my day any other way," I say with a small smile.

But deep in my mind, I still hear Jasmine's crying—the sound of half her heart breaking in that moment.

Chapter 14

The Midnight Tide keeps cutting through the North Atlantic, inching closer to the Caribbean Sea.

The North Atlantic is notorious for birthing fierce currents and slamming waves against rugged coastlines. Soon, though, it'll give way to the Caribbean's turquoise waters, sparkling around lush isles—from deep brooding blues to vibrant teals teeming with ocean life.

Most passengers find peace in this change. But not me.

Underneath all this luxury, a murder has taken place behind closed doors.

And I'm determined to dig up every clue I can, so when I face Jasper's family, my heart feels a little lighter.

Like Hansel and Gretel, the only trail of breadcrumbs we've got is left by Benson Wolf and Ida Birch.

An impatient debtor. An unforgiving ex-lover.

Both have reasons to kill Jasper.

But who had the guts to do it?

"Anything?" I ask Julia, who promised she'd keep an eye on Ida.

I spot the two of them near the poolside bar—Julia tucked under an umbrella, typing on her laptop, while Ida sips a tequila sunrise poolside, unbothered by the afternoon heat.

I want to tell Julia to wear something less bright than that lemony top and matching platforms—but knowing her, she probably doesn't own a neutral color in her closet. At least Ida doesn't seem fazed by Julia's presence, which means she hasn't been caught.

Julia sighs, scratching Rex's chin as he nudges her for attention. "So far? Nothing. Ida wandered the casino floor for a few hours, grabbed lunch with a friend, then came here. Pretty uneventful, honestly."

"So no red flags?" I press, hoping for more.

"Well, she's glued to her phone the whole time. Does that count?" Julia offers.

I chuckle, stepping out of the umbrella's shade. "Let me know if she does anything suspicious."

"Absolutely," Julia says. "Where to now?"

"To the security team," I reply. "Heard one of Cole's guys has been tailing Benson."

"Good luck with that," Julia calls as I wave and head back inside, the sun's glare less harsh behind the ship's walls. She adds, "See you later, Rex!"

Following Cole's text from minutes ago, Rex and I track down Pete, one of the security officers, lounging near the mini-golf course.

Curious, Rex sniffs along the hallways while I approach Pete, who's in his black uniform.

The mini-golf course is perched on the upper decks, dotted with miniature lighthouses and windmills. A fake river snakes through tricky water hazards. Fathers, kids, and bored grown men like Benson play against the ocean wind, but it looks as tedious as it sounds.

Spotting me, Pete straightens and meets me halfway. "Miss Dela Cruz, Mr. Hester said you'd be coming."

I glance at Benson. Blue putter in hand, he looks almost out of place. He's chatting with a dad, though their body language says they barely know each other.

I turn back to Pete. "Has Benson done anything suspicious?"

Lowering his voice like we're sharing a huge secret, Pete says, "At lunchtime, he went to reception asking for Jasper."

"He asked for Jasper?" I echo, surprised. That's bold. Almost like Benson wants us to know he's not hiding anything—or maybe he's trying to mislead us.

"He did," Pete nods. "I asked the receptionist how it went. First, Benson asked for Jasper's room number. When she refused, he asked her to call Jasper's room. She did. No answer. Benson looked annoyed for a moment, then just headed to the restaurant to eat."

I absorb it all, eyes flicking back to Benson. "Keep watching him. I want a full report on his day tonight. Thanks, Pete."

"You're welcome, Miss Dela Cruz," he says with a smile.

Benson isn't as stealthy as Ida when it comes to Jasper. That's progress, at least. But for now, nothing's certain.

We're swimming in speculation, not facts. But as long as we don't drown, we keep moving.

With that thought, Rex and I continue our afternoon hunt for clues—surveying the casino, hoping someone slips, or something slips out.

This is Jasper's turf. Maybe one of these guests is his boss, or at least the kind of people he runs with—if they don't hate him.

I can't tell Jasmine her brother's dead—not yet—and I definitely can't hit her with these harsh questions. So patience is my only weapon.

Hopefully, I'm less overwhelmed by the casino's flashing lights and overlapping noise this time. Even Rex pitches in, sitting alert beside me, watching every passerby like a loyal guard.

Jude checks in again. I can tell he's uncomfortable—like I'm a hawk circling for the first mistake.

"Are you sure there's nothing I can do for you, Miss Dela Cruz?" he asks for the second time today.

"Please, don't mind me," I say with a weak smile. "I'm sure you're busy. The tournament's still on for tonight, right?"

Jude nods. "With one less player, yeah. Mr. Thorne still isn't showing?"

Or ever.

I keep that to myself.

"No, he's not," I answer, sparing Jude the details.

He sighs softly. "If you need anything, just call, Miss Dela Cruz."

"Thanks," I say, leaning back against the wall, pretending to mind my own business while watching everyone else.

Every laugh, every conversation, I lean in closer, hoping to catch Jasper's name.

I glance at Rex, who's just as focused—maybe more. "Got anything, buddy?"

He looks up at me with those big, trusting eyes, but no clues yet.

A server hesitates, approaching me with a tray of hors d'oeuvres. "Shrimp tart?"

"I'm fine, thanks," I say, offering a small smile that he doesn't return. He just looks down and walks away, glancing back once before moving on to someone else.

I almost feel sorry for turning down his shrimp tarts—he seems genuinely upset.

But I have better things to do than nibble on mini tart shells filled with shrimp.

So instead of standing in one corner, Rex and I keep moving through the casino. I spot some of the poker players from last night and this morning, all absorbed in bets on baccarat and roulette.

Through the glass wall, the sun lowers, gold streaks melting over the horizon.

Rex and I circle the room dutifully as I slowly adjust to the overwhelming swirl of activity, flashing lights, and clattering sounds.

Then I see the young server again, standing at the far end of the aisle I'm in, seeming to debate whether to approach or retreat—like he's avoiding me.

It feels strange, but I don't dwell on it. Maybe he's just shy.

But even after I move to another spot, I can still feel his eyes on me—dark, round, curious... and maybe scared?

He avoids my gaze, but now I'm too bothered to let him blend into the crowd. Rex and I follow.

I weave through clusters of bystanders, watching some games unfold. Just before the server slips into the employee-only area, I tap his shoulder.

"Hey."

He flinches, slowly turning around. His gold name tag reads "Ericson."

Seeing me, Ericson pulls his nearly empty tray of shrimp tarts close, like shielding himself.

His voice trembles. "Yes, ma'am...?"

"Are you okay?" I ask, noticing sweat forming on his forehead and the white knuckles gripping his tray.

Ericson glances nervously around. "I'm fine."

Anyone can tell he isn't.

As another server passes by, I call out, "Excuse me? Can you take Ericson's tray for a moment? I need to speak to him privately."

Ericson looks surprised but doesn't refuse.

Once the other server takes the tray and walks off, I guide Ericson to a quieter corner.

"I'm not sure what's going on, but you don't seem well. How about taking an hour's rest? I'll talk to the manager to arrange it—"

"Please, no." Ericson touches my arm, then quickly pulls away. "I'm sorry, Miss Dela Cruz. I'm just... nervous."

"Nervous about what?" I press, watching him pick at dry skin on his thumb.

He hesitates, eyes darting around. When sure we're alone, he leans in and whispers, "I... I think I overheard something I shouldn't have last night."

My heart jumps.

Ericson continues, "It's about last night's winner at the poker tournament. I heard he was... threatened. Some guys were talking about it when I started my shift. His name is Jasper, right?"

He looks too shaky and honest to be making this up. I nod. "That's right—Jasper Thorne. What else did you hear?"

"Yes, in the men's room... last night." His voice falters, fear sharpening his gaze.

I quickly reassure him. "Ericson, don't worry about getting in trouble. Whatever you tell me stays between us. Since you heard Jasper was threatened, we need every detail for everyone's safety."

He nods, taking a shaky breath. "Two men were in the restroom saying they'd 'make Jasper pay.' That's what they said. I didn't think much of it until I learned something happened to a guy with the same name."

"So that's why you wanted to talk to me?" I soften, touched by his nervous honesty.

"Yes, ma'am," he admits. "I wasn't sure if I should say anything..."

"You did the right thing." I give his forearm a brief squeeze. "Can you help us more by identifying them? Do you remember what they looked like?"

Ericson nods, more confident. "I was cleaning the restroom, so I got a good look."

"Are they here now?" I ask, eyes scanning the crowd.

He squints, darting his eyes. Then shakes his head. "Not seeing them."

"But you'd recognize them?"

"I think so."

"Were they players in the tournament?"

"Yes!" Ericson says firmly. "I saw them on the screens during the tournament."

I pull out my phone and pull up the recording of last night's tournament on The Midnight Tide's website. I play a clip showing all players seated at the poker table, including Jasper.

Avoiding Jasper's face—just the sight tightens my chest—I turn the screen toward Ericson.

"Which ones?"

He studies the paused video, then points to two men sitting side by side. "These two. I'm sure—they seemed close from what I overheard."

I look at the screen. I don't recall seeing either at breakfast.

Turning the screen back toward me, I read the names below the video, left to right from the dealer.

Those two are Chase Ford and Joe Booker.

Could they be the new key suspects?

One can only hope—and I really hope so.

Chapter 15

Gone too soon are the fleeting colors that just bathed The Midnight Tide. The oranges and purples of sunset have slipped away, replaced by a deep blue sky sprinkled with stars.

But from the casino, those stars hardly matter... not when everyone's eyes are locked on the prize.

As for me, my eyes are fixed on finding Chase Ford and Joe Booker.

Thanks to Ericson and his sharp ears, the lines he caught last night—"making Jasper pay"—could just mean debts, but they could also be a warning. A threat of murder.

I'm not taking chances. I'm chasing every lead I can.

On our way out, I tap Jude's shoulder. "Hey, have you seen Chase Ford and Joe Booker? They're two of the tournament players from last night."

Jude barely scrunches his face, but he knows exactly who I mean. "Oh, Mr. Ford and Mr. Booker? I saw them earlier today playing blackjack, but they left hours ago."

"Where to?"

"Don't know, Miss Dela Cruz."

"And are they in tonight's tournament?"

He checks his clipboard, scanning the player list. "No, they didn't register."

"Alright, thanks. Keep an eye out, will you?"

"Got it, Miss Dela Cruz." Jude tosses me a casual two-finger salute.

Rex and I step out, and I pull out my radio. "Julia? Send a photo of two passengers—Chase Ford and Joe Booker. Beta, if you're listening, I need your team to find them ASAP."

"Copy that, Rose," Cole's voice cuts through.

A crackle, then Julia replies, "On it, Miss Dela Cruz."

Rex and I hit the decks, scanning the promenade, dining hall, restaurants, cafés, bars, lounges... nothing.

An hour ticks by. Security fans out—checking rooms, roaming halls, cruising the casino.

At 8:00 p.m., someone's combing the library, the internet café, even the bridge wing.

Still nothing.

No one reports seeing them.

The ship pulses with life, every inch decked out and buzzing with guests—but without Chase and Joe, it suddenly feels huge. Empty.

Two men don't just vanish, do they?

My mind races through darker scenarios—kidnapped, tossed overboard, or worse.

Then Cole's voice comes over the radio. "Rose? We found them. Just got out of the theater."

Relief crashes over me like a cold wind down my spine.

"Take them to the conference room, will you?" I say, feet scraping the marble in the lobby. Rex's paws barely whisper behind me. "I'm on my way."

I don't waste a second.

The conference room clock reads 8:34 p.m. as I walk in.

Ben and Cole sit two men at the glass table—medium build, one brown-haired, the other black, one wearing glasses.

Rex and I slip in just as one man asks, "Why are we here again?"

Ben's eyes find me before I say a word. "Just in time. Miss Dela Cruz wants to have a word."

The men glance at me, annoyance and curiosity mixed on their faces.

Cole points. "That's Joe Booker." Then nods at the other. "And Chase Ford."

Chase scowls. "And what do you need from us?"

"Please, have a seat first." I gesture to the chairs and circle around to Ben.

Ben pulls out a chair, letting me sit. Joe, calmer, drops into a seat right away. Chase hesitates a moment longer, then follows.

"Thank you." I smile, building rapport for now—dropping the heavy questions later. "I'm sure you're wondering why you're here. Let me get straight to it..."

I lay out the usual line: Jasper was threatened last night. We're looking into it. Then I add, "Someone overheard you at the casino—something about making Jasper pay. Care to explain?"

Chase sighs like he's been stuck here too long—though it's only been minutes.

Joe keeps his expression flat. "Yeah. For cheating. Heard he was cheating at the tournament."

"Allegedly," I say. "Our team hasn't confirmed that."

Joe shrugs. "Well, we know."

Chase jumps in, irritated. "Someone should make him pay for cheating, right?"

I watch them closely. Neither gives much away—not even Chase, who's clearly itching to leave. "So, you threatened him?"

Chase snickers, leaning back. "No. Thought about it, but figured it'd be a waste of breath."

Cole cuts in, arms crossed. "You didn't even pay him a visit last night? Give him your two cents on cheating?"

"Waste of breath," Chase repeats.

"We barely know the guy," Joe adds. "Would be weird to visit his room. Don't even know where it is."

Joe states it like it's obvious—as if the sea being salty or the sky being blue.

Still, I size them up, shoulder to shoulder, scanning for the possibility they're two of the five hooded men.

Remembering those numbers reminds me just how far off we are in this investigation.

Not one of them confirmed.

Setting the pressure aside, I press on. "So, let me be clear, Mr. Ford and Mr. Booker. You're telling us you don't know Mr. Thorne, that you were just badmouthing him for allegedly cheating, and you didn't see him after the tournament?"

"Exactly." Chase snaps his fingers, sharp as a whip.

Joe pauses, reading between my lines, and nods. "That's the gist of it. Honestly, we only heard stories about Jasper before the tournament. And, you know, emotions run high in high-stakes poker. Chase and I were just venting after losing thousands last night. Said some careless things. That's all."

Joe's calmness almost sells me on it. But with my experience in murder investigations, trust doesn't come easy. Traitors only betray if you trust them first.

I want to ask more, but honestly, there's little to go on—only what Ericson overheard. Neither denies the conversation happened.

They just shrug it off like it's nothing.

Is it really nothing?

Are they that calm because they had no part in Jasper's death, no clue at all? Or are they... sociopaths? Emotionless killers who don't care if Jasper lived or died?

Either way, I can't hold them here on a whisper of suspicion when we need a mountain of proof.

As if reading my thoughts, Chase asks, "So, can we leave now?"

I glance at Ben and Cole. They want to keep talking but see no reason to hold them.

Ben makes the call. "Sure. Thank you for your time, Mr. Ford... Mr. Booker."

With a nod from Ben, Chase and Joe rise like the chairs are on fire.

Joe nods at us; Chase moves straight for the door.

I don't feel good about how that went. If I want them back, I better find something to make that happen.

Before anyone can say a word, Julia comes barreling down the hall, ignoring Chase and Joe, racing to us.

I jump up as Cole opens the door for a breathless Julia.

"What?" I ask, throat tightening. That look on her face—trouble. I don't like it.

She swallows hard; a bead of sweat rolls down her forehead. "You need to come quick. Ida Birch is causing a scene outside Jasper's room."

No time to react. Rex bolts ahead, leash bouncing wildly.

Julia follows without waiting for me.

We rush out of the conference room, racing to the upper deck. The hallway, usually calm and peaceful, tonight throbs with drunken screams and murmurs from a crowd gathered outside Jasper's door.

Cole leaps up and runs straight into the chaos.

There's Ida Birch, flushed and drunk, pounding the door, yelling, "All I ever did was love you! How could you do this to me? Come on out!"

"Miss Birch." Cole grabs her arm, but she shoves him off with surprising strength.

Gasps ripple through the crowd as Cole stumbles back, shocked.

I step in, gripping Ida's arms. "Ida, stop this."

Her glassy eyes don't meet mine. She doesn't even hear me. She yanks one arm free, lunging at the door again, but Julia catches the flailing limb.

Ida wiggles free, cursing and calling for Jasper as we drag her away. One heel falls off like a drunken Cinderella.

I glance at the crowd. Some worried, some just watching for gossip.

As Julia and I struggle with Ida's weight, she grows heavier, almost dragging us down.

Then Ben steps in, lifting her in his arms with a quick breath. He looks... heroic, carrying a damsel in distress in his crisp uniform.

But beyond the image, Ida is out cold. Her head bobs with every step.

It's barely nine, and she's drunk asleep, professing love ... to a dead man.

Does she know? My heart tightens at the thought.

We escort her back to her room. That question lingers, just like the strong smell of booze on Ida—the woman who can't give us the answers we need.

Chapter 16

"How is she?" I tap Julia's shoulder as she peers inside the dining hall, watching Ida and her friend help themselves to the breakfast buffet among the teeming passengers and scrambling servers.

I can only imagine how brutal Ida's hangover must be after passing out at nine last night, but if she's up this early—7:00 a.m. on the dot—it can't be that bad. Yet those ridiculous sunglasses hiding her eyes as she picks fruit for her yogurt tell a different story.

Julia perks up when she spots me and Rex. Like always, she acknowledges Rex first, scratching behind his ear with a soft, "Good morning, buddy."

Rex wags his tail and stands on his hind legs, thrilled. Around us, the entire ship stirs awake, sunlight glittering over the ocean like a promise of the day ahead.

Because at exactly eight, we dock in Amber Cove.

I wait out Julia and Rex's brief reunion, then she turns to me. "I've been watching her a while. She's just... hungover."

"I can tell," I say. "Heard anything about last night's... incident?"

The embarrassing, drunken mess, if I'm being honest.

Julia shakes her head.

She's taken her watch on Ida seriously since yesterday, and I admire her dedication. The Midnight Tide is busier than usual, with a few people under close watch—Ida, Benson, Chase, Joe.

And somehow, the list keeps growing... without a shred of real evidence.

For now, I tell myself.

Julia adds, "So far, Ida's only complained about a headache and wanting to skip the Amber Cove tour, nothing about her little stunt last night."

"Think she remembers?" I ask, eyes on the pair as they shuffle toward the juice dispensers.

"If I were her, I'd refuse to remember," Julia says with a small, knowing smile.

The ship edges closer to port, and my heart starts pounding in my chest.

A thousand thoughts whirl through my mind, but one stands out—Jasmine. In an hour or two, I'll be sitting across from her, handing out more heartbreak than comfort.

Before I can brace for that emotional storm, Julia nudges me sharply.

I snap out of my daze and spot Ida being half-dragged toward us by her friend Alice—the same one we met last night in their double deluxe suite.

"I don't want to..." Ida mumbles, barely resisting as Alice hauls her closer.

Soon, they stand in front of us, plates half-full. Alice offers a tight smile. "Rose, right? We met last night... in a rather embarrassing situation."

She tugs Ida's arm, urging her to say something. Ida clearly doesn't want to talk, but with Alice glaring daggers, she mutters, "I'm sorry, I guess... for... whatever I did last night."

Since she's here, I seize the moment. "You don't remember, do you?"

Ida rolls her eyes, not meeting my gaze. If only I could see those eyes behind those dark sunglasses. "Alice jogged my memory earlier, but... I can't say I remember everything."

Before I can say anything, Ida stomps like a spoiled kid hearing no. "Can we just drop it? I don't want to talk about it. I was drunk, and I didn't mean any of it."

To me, it sounds like Ida's wrestling with a lot of unresolved feelings for Jasper—feelings she can't fix anymore and will have to move past on her own.

Still, I'm tempted to ask if she knows what happened to Jasper—if she has any clue. But given how she drunkenly stumbled over here demanding Jasper come to the door, she probably doesn't know much.

Why else would she go knocking on a dead man's door? Surely not to make peace with his ghost, right?

But what if she did?

I nod at her, her face flushed with shame. "We'll pretend it never happened, Miss Birch."

Ida shrugs and tosses her hair back. As she leaves, Alice lingers for a moment. "I promise I'll keep her in line for the rest of the cruise."

I chuckle. "Thank you."

Alice trails behind Ida, who's scolding her for dragging her into this.

Watching them, the pit in my stomach only grows. Ida's involvement is still unclear, but her motive is obvious. I tell Julia, "You're going to have to follow them in Amber Cove, okay? Make sure they come back to the ship."

"Oh, absolutely. Don't worry." Julia waves a casual hand. "I even have my disguise picked out."

I can't help but eye her lime-green shirt dress. "Is it less colorful than that? They might spot you easily if you wear anything neon."

Julia stifles a laugh. "If you must know, it's blue—not neon."

"Okay, blue's good," I say, winking.

After that quick check-in with Julia, I head to Cole's office to arrange security tails on Benson, Chase, and Joe, just in case they head ashore as we near port.

As The Midnight Tide glides into the Bay of Puerto Plata, the once-distant shoreline bursts into view—lush hills spilling down to ivory beaches. Even the air feels different here—thicker with foliage and blooms.

Inside Cole's office, Stacy sits beside him, greeting me immediately. "Hey there."

"Excited to see land after two days?" I tease.

She grins. "Yeah, but my boyfriend here has other plans." Stacy shoots a playful scowl at Cole, who looks up from his phone.

"I swear I didn't force your sister to come with me," Cole says. "If anything, she insisted on joining the local enforcement coordination."

And transporting Jasper's body, I think grimly. I know the drill too well.

"I just didn't want him to be lonely." Stacy smiles softly.

"Well, you won't be stuck with the police all day, Stace," I say. "There's a nice date waiting for you once this is over."

Her smile fades fast as she asks, "And you? You're meeting Jasper's sister today, right?"

My heart skips. I don't show it, only nod. "Yeah. Ben and Rex are coming too."

The look in Stacy's eyes tells me she's about to ask how I feel about meeting Jasmine, but I don't want to go there. I might just freak myself out. So, I switch gears quickly. "Anyway, Cole, have you assigned your men to tail Benson, Chase, and Joe?"

"I have," Cole says. "They'll follow them as soon as we hit port. And Ida?"

"Julia will be right behind her," I answer. Then add, "Though I ran into her half an hour ago, and she says she doesn't remember what she did last night."

"Doesn't or doesn't want to?" Cole tilts his head, making me snort.

"I don't know—but I do know she still has feelings for Jasper, okay?"

Stacy pipes up, "Strong feelings that could've turned murderous?"

"Um..." I pause to think. "She doesn't always seem sensible, so who knows? Maybe she let her emotions do the thinking."

"That's why we have to keep an eye on all of them. Everyone's emotional—whether it's love or money," Cole replies just as his phone buzzes with a new message. "Anyway, the police are already waiting at the port."

"You sure you don't need Ben and me to help?" I ask, maybe stalling. Meeting Jasmine feels like a mountain I don't want to climb just yet.

"Stacy and I got this," Cole assures me.

Stacy briefly reaches out and squeezes my arm. "You should worry about Jasmine first."

"Okay, then." I head for the door, taking Stacy's advice. I can't be more of a mess than Jasmine, right? "See you later."

Stacy waves goodbye to Rex and me as I step out, the warm breeze hitting my face and sending chills through me.

"I can handle this, right, Rex?" I ask my dog, who matches my slow pace.

Rex looks up and gives a firm bark.

"Thanks, bud," I say, eyes scanning the nearby port. Beyond it, a kaleidoscope of brightly painted buildings cling to the lush hillsides, their colors popping against towering palms and thick overgrowth.

Under the clear water, glimpses of coral reefs decorate the ocean floor—promises of sun-drenched adventures.

At least for the passengers.

For me, the gnawing fear of facing Jasmine's heartbreak reignites something dark—a hollow regret I'm not sure I can fill. No matter what anyone says, I keep thinking... I could've stopped Jasper's death if I'd gone after him that night.

Now, I have to pretend I did everything I could—right in front of Jasmine.

That thought makes me want to throw up.

Still, I take my time walking around the ship, dreading the creaks and groans as we inch closer to port.

But reality only waits so long before it catches up.

Chapter 17

The eighty-something-degree heat in Cap-Haïtien makes me sweat despite the gentle sea breeze that tries to temper it. I could blame the sun's glare, but I know it's my nerves betraying me.

Right now, Ben, Rex, and I are on our way to Jasmine's hotel.

Nothing about the bright day, the refreshing gusts of wind, or the pleasantly humid air distracts me from the knot twisting tighter in my stomach.

The path to the hotel—just a few blocks from the port—smells like tropical flowers. Charming buildings and quaint shops line the streets, their colorful facades contrasting and complementing the lush greenery spilling over every corner. Overhead, mountain ranges bask in sunlight.

This is the kind of place people pay to visit. And here I am, barely able to appreciate it.

Ben takes my hand as we walk deeper into the street. Rex strides beside me, casting quick glances my way, like he's checking if I'm holding up.

"Are you ready?" Ben asks.

Knowing I'm not—and probably never will be—I still manage a smile. "I have to be."

"Don't worry, I'm here for you," Ben says, lifting my hand to his lips and pressing a gentle kiss to it.

"I know," I say, comforted by his calm.

Soon, we reach the hotel we booked for Jasmine just yesterday. It's another eye-catching building, with a thatched roof and a panoramic balcony overlooking the ocean. It feels both cultural and elegant. Even the lobby, filled with wooden furniture, glass accents, and splashes of vibrant color, stays true to the theme.

Still, no matter how impressive the architecture or interior, my nerves won't loosen their grip. If my hands weren't full—Ben holding one, the other gripping Rex's leash—I'd probably be rubbing them raw.

That anxious.

Ben, as casual as ever and seemingly untouched by nerves, follows the signs to the open-air restaurant.

Any minute now, I'll see Jasmine—and my heart will drop like a pirate walking the plank.

For now, I focus on the restaurant itself: walls made of woven bamboo, tables carved from driftwood, chairs inspired by palm leaves. The floor's a mosaic of seashells, and colorful artwork hangs on the already beautiful walls.

It doesn't take long to spot Jasmine. She's definitely the blonde woman sitting alone in the corner, a handkerchief pressed to her nose.

She's crying on her own.

For a moment, I want to stop dead, maybe take a breath—and throw up my guts. But Ben and Rex keep me moving. I force one foot in front of the other until we reach her table.

Seeing her up close, my chest tightens.

Jasmine looks so much like Jasper. Of course—twins. But the last time I saw Jasper's face, he was pale and bluish, with those eerie golden chips in his eyes.

Staring at Jasmine pulls me back to that exact moment.

I freeze for a second—then Ben's touch nudges me forward.

Jasmine's already watching us, her face tear-streaked, nose red and swollen.

"Jasmine Thorne?" I say at last, my mind flickering with images of Jasper.

She nods weakly. "That's me. Are you Rose? From The Midnight Tide?"

"Yes," I say, pointing to Ben. "And this is Ben Anderson, the captain."

Jasmine rises to greet us properly, but I wave her off, settling into the chairs across from her. "No, please. Stay seated, Jasmine."

She collapses back with a tired thud, like that simple movement drained her last ounce of energy. Maybe it did. Maybe she's been running on empty since I broke the news.

We sit. Jasmine lifts her handkerchief from her lap and wipes her face.

"I'm so sorry we have to meet like... this."

"Don't worry. We completely understand," I say with a gentle smile.

But she doesn't meet it. Her eyes stay glued behind us, fixed on the sea.

I glance over my shoulder and see the port—The Midnight Tide gleaming in the sunlight, like it wasn't Jasper's final destination.

I turn back to Jasmine. "First, I want to say how sorry we are for your loss. Our company is working closely with the police."

"You said he was... killed?" Jasmine finally meets my eyes, glassy and drained. "Did you find who did it?"

The question hits me like a splash of cold water.

There it is—the guilt ready to paralyze me and leave me tongue-tied.

"We, uh, we're still..." I falter.

Ben cuts in. "We have a few suspects, and we're investigating closely."

"And who are they?" Jasmine turns to him.

From under the table, Ben squeezes my hand. "Miss Dela Cruz here can brief you. She's been working tirelessly on this case and knows every detail."

My heart swells. Leave it to Ben to remind me how capable I am.

Following his lead, I say, "Right now, we're focused on four people. Maybe you can tell us if any names sound familiar."

Jasmine nods once.

I continue. "First, Benson Wolf—Jasper owed him money. Benson even admitted to following Jasper on the cruise to collect."

I pause, looking for a reaction, but Jasmine says nothing.

"There's also Ida Birch. She claims to be an ex-girlfriend. Do you know her?"

Jasmine's brow furrows. "Ex-girlfriend? No. If they were serious, I'd know her name."

Huh. So they weren't serious... then why did Ida react like they were?

I press on. "Then two poker players: Chase Ford and Joe Booker. A casino employee overheard them talking about making Jasper pay. Do you know either?"

The line between Jasmine's eyebrows deepens as frustration wells up in her. "I don't recognize any of those names."

Ben's voice softens with understanding. "That's okay. We don't expect you to have all the answers right now, Jasmine. We know this is hard."

I add, "If it's too much, you can rest for a few hours. We can—"

"No," Jasmine cuts in sharply. "I want this nightmare over."

The quiver in her voice betrays real pain. I'm sure the last thing she wants is to sit here talking about the people who probably murdered her brother. But maybe this is the only way forward—the hardest, but the only way.

I realize she doesn't need comfort or apologies. She needs help. So I push past my own feelings and get to work.

"Well then," I say, "we have a few more questions that might help us understand this... murder. What can you tell us about Jasper? Why would someone plan something so vicious?"

Jasmine swallows hard. I see her throat move—more tears, probably. "Jasper had a lot of enemies—people he owed money to, people he ran from. He was addicted to gambling... and money. But I never thought it'd get this bad."

"What do you mean?" I press, watching her face twist in sadness, haunted by old memories.

She hesitates. "We've been getting threats for months. They came to our house—harassed Jasper, harassed us—to get their money. They'd egg the place, throw rocks.

Once, someone beat him in a parking lot. It got so bad Jasper left home. I haven't seen him in a long time."

Her voice breaks, a small whimper escaping like she's already mourning a loss she can't undo.

A sinking feeling settles in my gut. I push it down.

Jasmine pulls herself together. "Since then, Jasper moved around—different casinos, different cities—to avoid these people. Maybe they found him... on the ship."

Her gaze drifts to the horizon, longing and grief swirling like a brewing storm that could tear The Midnight Tide apart.

If she feels that way, I can't blame her.

But I can help her. I have to find who did this.

"So these adversaries... you don't know who they are?" I ask.

"No," she says. "Jasper did everything to keep us out of his mess. Leaving home was his first move—to protect us."

Ben and I exchange a glance, a mix of disappointment and understanding passing between us.

Rex whimpers softly and stretches on the floor, sensing our frustration with so little to go on.

I press on, searching for the next thread: Jasper's boss.

"Does Jasper work for anyone? We checked his phone and found a contact saved as 'Boss.' Maybe you can help us figure out who that is."

"Boss?" Jasmine repeats, confused, then her eyes widen like a memory just clicked. "I'm not sure, but I've heard of someone like that."

"Who?" I lean forward, eager.

She hesitates, then shakes off the doubt. "I don't know his real name. He goes by a codename."

"That helps," I say, grasping for any lifeline to keep me afloat before I drown in defeat.

Jasmine breathes in deeply, shaky. "The poker community calls him The Ace."

"The Ace?" The name tastes sharp on my tongue.

Jasmine nods. "Jasper said he's a notorious card shark. Skilled but cheats to win. Before Jasper left, he told me he was going to find this Ace."

Could Jasper have found him? Worked for him? Crossed him? The name alone sends a chill down my spine.

New player. New suspect. New motive.

New answers to find.

Chapter 18

After leaving Jasmine at the police station so she could finally see Jasper's body, the weight on my shoulders barely lifts—maybe half as much. It feels like Jasper's ghost is still riding on my back, haunting me, begging me to find out who did this.

Now, we have a new lead—a name I hope finally takes us somewhere. But following this trail of breadcrumbs isn't as satisfying as *getting the cake*, whatever that metaphor really means.

Ben and Rex have been quietly keeping me company since we left Jasmine.

The three of us navigate the crowded streets back toward the port, tuning out the bartering cries of locals hawking their goods, the distant beat of drums from a street performance, even the sharp calls of exotic birds darting overhead.

Under the relentless heat, Ben suddenly pulls me toward a nearby ice cream shop. "Come on, a little treat might cheer you up, don't you think?"

He doesn't wait for an answer, steering Rex and me toward the small shop with its blinking neon sign and a line of customers snaking out the door.

"Don't you think we should head back to the ship instead?" I ask, brows furrowing, sweat beading at my hairline. My appetite? Not exactly craving sweets.

Ben flashes that roguish grin of his—the one that says he's only slightly breaking the plan. "A little detour won't hurt. It's still early, and the city's alive."

As he pulls me deeper into the queue, the sweet scent of fresh fruit and cream curls around me. The shop's air conditioning offers a welcome break from the tropical heat.

I know why he wants me here, and I can't help but smile. Grateful, really, that he's looking out for me. Even I can't explain the mood swings of my own restless mind. Instead of dwelling, I loop my arm through his and match his enthusiasm. "I'll get the strawberry."

Ben smiles back. "You get us a table. I'll grab the desserts. And whipped cream for Rex?"

Rex wags his tail excitedly and barks once.

"That's a yes," I say.

While Ben waits in line, Rex and I slip outside to a table shaded by a striped umbrella.

"Come on, buddy." I pat my lap. Rex hops up, leaning his front paws on me. Then I lift him onto the chair beside me.

He settles in his yellow chair as I lean back, watching the slow rhythm of the city unfold. Locals treat this morning like any other; tourists snap photos, laugh, chatter.

The world keeps spinning, oblivious to anyone's tragedy—even if it stopped for Jasmine and her family.

Maybe for me, too.

But the world keeps turning for people like Benson, Ida, Chase, Joe—and *The Ace*.

Right. That thought makes me pull my phone from my pocket. The sleek device hums warm in my hand, alive with possibility—like the answer to *The Ace's* identity.

My fingers fly across the screen, typing "The Ace" and "card shark" into the search bar like it's my last chance.

I want to know who this man really is.

From the little Jasmine's told us, The Ace sounds like someone at the heart of this poker crime. She didn't call him "notorious" for nothing.

Could he be the missing link? The one who holds all the answers?

I hope so, as my screen lights up with results—none promising.

The first few explain "card shark"—a skilled or deceptive card player who makes money at games like poker. The word comes from "card sharp." Not that I needed to know that.

There are a few video tutorials on becoming a card shark, too. Not helpful.

Then come pictures of the ace from a deck of cards.

A book called *Astounding Aces*. A mobile poker game.

The more I scroll, the more my face tightens with disappointment. Finding this guy won't be easy. His reputation is solid—and so is his method for hiding his identity. It's all part of the brand.

Just then, Ben returns, balancing a tray loaded with ice cream scoops and a cup of whipped cream. He spots me staring at my phone. "Anything interesting over there?"

"I was looking up 'The Ace.'" I sigh, setting my phone down. "Don't be mad—I know you wanted a little ice cream date."

Ben gently sets the tray on the table and sits beside me. "I love you too much to get mad over that. So, spill it. What did you find?"

He hands me my strawberry ice cream and nudges the whipped cream toward Rex. My dog wastes no time, standing on his chair and diving in.

Ben and I laugh. Unknowingly, he just made me blush.

Distracted for a moment, I answer, "Not much. This is one of those cases where you have to scour the entire internet for the right clue—if you find him at all."

I take a spoonful of ice cream, watching Ben enjoy his pistachio.

He says, "How about I help? We can stay a while."

I squint playfully. "You sure? If you want to wander the city, I won't complain."

Ben smirks. "I think you'd mind. If we go on a quick date, you'll still be thinking about this case. Not that I'm complaining—that's the life dating a PI."

I huff at the tease, a reminder of old times. "That was before. Now, I'm a cruise director."

"Who still investigates," he reminds me with a smile.

"It's a curse," I say, picking up my phone again.

Ben pulls out his phone, too. We slowly eat melting ice cream, searching for The Ace together.

This time, I add "notorious" and "poker" to the search.

The new results point to car sharks—fictional vehicles, some shark movies, and ocean encounter videos.

Still, I scroll every page, hunting for the right result, but it's no use.

Ben is just as absorbed in his phone; his eyebrows furrow as he struggles to uncover The Ace's identity on the supposedly all-knowing internet.

Half an hour slips by like a wick burning fast. I still haven't found anything on The Ace, so I ask, "Anything?"

Ben barely looks up, focused. "Well, right now I'm reading a list of card sharks starting with Victor Lassere in the 1920s."

A video on how to be a card shark plays muted on my phone. The guy in it looks far from notorious—more like a high schooler who probably isn't even allowed in casinos yet.

I reply, "Try someone from the twenty-first century."

"On it, Boss." Ben winks, scrolling again.

My half-melted ice cream turns into sticky goop, but I ignore it, juggling words in the search bar, reshuffling, adding new terms. I sift through every result, skimming articles and video descriptions, just to be sure.

Minutes stretch into an hour.

Ben and I sit glued to our phones, like hypnotized by the glow of our screens.

The feeling of defeat starts creeping in. Are we really going to find The Ace this way? If not, how? Jasmine said The Ace is Jasper's boss, but we've only assumed he's on the ship—along with five hundred other passengers.

Finding a man who wants to stay anonymous in a crowd is impossible.

But maybe... all we can do is wait.

Scrolling mindlessly, my eye catches an online forum from a year ago. Under "Urban Legends & Lost People," a thread titled: *Card Shark The Ace. Anyone Seen Him?*

Finally, the words I've hunted for blink back at me.

I click, silently praying this is the clue we need.

The thread's started by "Shadow Walker 87," who writes: *Anyone heard about a new card shark called "The*

Ace?" *Dude's like a ghost—vanishes after cleaning out casino poker tables. Last spotted in Vegas, then poof... gone.*

"Lucky Lady 13" replies: *People in the gambling scene talk about him! Never loses, never caught. Creepy.*

I read on, hoping for facts, not gossip.

Someone calls The Ace a hustler and cheat. Another calls him a "glitch" and a "whisper in the code." Shadow insists The Ace is a mind reader who knows your cards before you do.

At first, it seems like casual chatter, but then someone asks: *If The Ace is so great, is there proof he's real? No one even knows his real name.*

My breath hitches reading the next reply.

"Card Reader 4 Life" writes: *I think I know him. My gramps played with him a few months ago—got him to sit down for drinks.*

"Who is it? Spill!" Shadow demands.

I hold my breath as if I'm watching live messages, not reading a year-old thread.

"Card Reader 4 Life" answers: *Gramps says his name is Max Parrish.*

A shudder escapes me.

I'm sure I've seen that name before...

To be certain, I open my email where Julia sent the cruise's confirmed passenger list.

Blood rushes in my ears.

Nothing else matters—Ben's curious glance, Rex napping beside me, the blurred crowd, the sun and sea—all fade.

My full focus is on my phone as the list loads.

Once it's up, my thumb races down the alphabet to the Ps.

There: Max Parrish.

I stare, disbelief crashing over me. The Ace is onboard The Midnight Tide.

Was Jasper working under Max Parrish? The "boss" we've been chasing? Were they partners in card counting, cheating? Was Max helping Jasper from the ship while Jasper paid him?

It would explain The Ace calling Jasper about winnings the night after Jasper's death.

It all fits. Now I just have to confirm it.

Ben reads the change in my face and finally asks, "Did you find him?"

"Yes," I say, relief thick in my voice. "The Ace—Max Parrish—is a passenger on this cruise."

Ben's face tightens—almost constipated.

"What?" I say. "This is good, right?"

He pauses, his gaze turning worried. "It's good news, Rose, but... the timing worries me."

"What do you mean?" The words slip out as the realization hits.

Of course.

We're in Amber Cove.

Passengers have disembarked... and Max Parrish could have, too. No security on him. If he's involved in Jasper's death, he might not come back.

"Well, crap..." is all I manage to say.

Chapter 19

"He's going to come back to the ship, right?" I ask Ben for the ninth time since we got back to The Midnight Tide and confirmed Max Parrish isn't on board.

The thought of Max—aka The Ace—slipping through the city's fingers sends bile rising to my throat. It's a sick twist to have found him... only to risk losing him now.

We're standing in the reception area. The ship rocks gently with the calm sea, and the crystal chandelier above the grand stairs sways with a slow, hypnotic rhythm.

The receptionist barely glances up, her eyes glued to the computer screen.

Ben stays calm, leaning against a decorative pillar, watching me pace. Rex curls up at his feet, loyal as ever. The gangway remains open behind us, welcoming passengers on and off.

"If Max's clean," Ben says, eyes steady on me, "he'll come back. Remember that call he made to Jasper right after the incident? Sounds like he's still in the dark."

"Right?" I cling to Ben's words, though my gaze keeps flicking down to the port, hoping Max Parrish will appear early.

I've checked his passenger file; now I know exactly who we're watching for. For someone notorious in the poker world, Max's brown hair, green eyes, and sharp features don't fit the usual villain image. He looks like he just stepped out of college. But appearances can lie.

Especially if he's been wiping poker tables clean.

"Calm down, will you?" Ben's voice is low, soothing as he steps away from the wall and closes the gap between us. The reception is empty, so he doesn't hesitate—wraps me in a steady embrace. Normally, I'd protest. But right now? I need it. I let him.

Then a familiar voice cuts through the quiet, clearing her throat: "The passengers might start rumors if the ship's captain is dating the cruise director."

I pull back, spotting Stacy and Cole standing in the entryway. Stacy's grinning, eyes sparkling with mischief—but half her attention's on Rex, who greets her like an old friend.

I roll my eyes. "And you're dating the head of security."

Stacy takes Cole's hand, lifting it dramatically. "Guilty as charged."

"So, how's the city?" I ask Stacy. It's only early afternoon, but she clearly hasn't been out exploring much.

"Oh, it's just too hot," she shrugs, crouching to pet Rex some more.

Cole explains, watching Stacy with a knowing look, "I asked if she wanted to check out the city a bit, but she said no. I think she's just... emotional after seeing Jasmine earlier at the station."

Of course. Stacy witnessed Jasmine's first look at Jasper's lifeless body in months—at the morgue. I can't imagine how brutal that must've been.

I study Stacy's face, searching for any sign of it. She hides it well—too well. She won't admit it, but this is hitting her hard. Still, she manages a brave smile as she pets Rex. "Well, it was a heart-wrenching scene, okay? Right, Rex?"

"I get you." I wink. Stacy smiles back, and Rex leans into her knee, licking her chin like he agrees.

Ben's tone shifts, sharp and serious. "What did the authorities say, Cole?"

Cole pulls away from the warmth of the moment, stepping into his professional mode. "Investigation's ongoing, but they've cleared us to keep working onboard—so long as we update them on anything new."

"Of course," I say, automatic.

"They've confirmed Jasper's cause of death," Cole lowers his voice even more, barely audible over the distant hum of ships and busy port workers. "Like Dr. Bates said—strangulation. They're running more tests—checking for DNA we might've missed, tissue under fingernails, that kind of thing."

"Good. I'm glad the police are thorough." I nod, trying to feel reassured. "Wish we could've handed them a more... precise suspect list."

"They trust what we've got so far," Cole says firmly. "They've heard of you, Rose. Confident you can crack this case without their hands-on help."

My eyes widen. "They... what?"

Ben nudges me, pride shining through his smile. "News travels fast. The Midnight Tide's had its share of drama, but you're known for getting results."

"Oh, please. Don't flatter me," I mutter, cheeks heating.

"I'm just saying," Ben insists.

I glare, but teasing. "And no need to say it again."

Stacy stands, scanning the quiet reception. Aside from the windows, floral arrangements, and cruise posters, it's nothing flashy. She asks, "Why are you here, anyway?"

I glance at Ben. "We're... waiting for a passenger to come back."

Stacy arches an eyebrow; Cole looks curious, too.

"And who's this important passenger?" Stacy presses.

"Max Parrish," I say, swallowing nerves. "He might've been Jasper's boss... known in the poker scene as The Ace."

"A skilled card shark," Ben adds.

Stacy blinks, processing. "You mean someone who counts cards to cheat?"

"Among other things," I reply. I'm still piecing together how The Ace pulls off his tricks. Maybe he'll tell us.

I continue, "Max and Jasper came here together. Max helped Jasper cheat and win—and then called him the next day to collect his cut of the quarter-million pot."

"That sounds plausible." Stacy doesn't hide her surprise.

But Cole cuts in, his mind working. "Are we sure Max didn't take the money himself—and kill Jasper? That call could be a setup to seem innocent."

My knees nearly give out at Cole's suggestion.

Of course, I've thought the same thing myself, but I want to cling to the more optimistic side. Right now, all we have are dead ends—like mice trapped in a maze, none of us sure which way to turn.

"I, uh..." I stammer, then blurt out the one hope I have. "I hope that's not the case."

"So that's why you're waiting here." Stacy reads me like a book. "You have a feeling he's not coming back?"

I slump back, letting the weight of worry press down. "What if he doesn't? What if we found him a few hours too late? I really think Max Parrish could turn this case around."

Stacy checks her watch. "Passengers have four hours left in the city. Maybe Max is just one of those guys who wants to enjoy his vacation to the fullest. How about I distract you while we wait?"

Cole adds quickly, "I'll talk to the receptionist, get them to notify us when Max returns. I'll have some men search around town, too—so you can breathe easier."

"You'll do that?" The tight knot in my chest loosens just a little.

Stacy pulls me close. "Of course he will. And I've been wanting to try the hot stone massage on this cruise. Come with me?"

"I don't think a spa will help when my brain's racing," I say honestly.

But Ben chimes in, insisting, "You should go with Stacy, Rose. We won't have much to do until all the suspects are back."

"Yeah, I know, but—" I start to argue.

"No more buts." Stacy pulls me up the stairs. "It's settled—you're getting pampered."

As she drags me away, I call back to Ben, who's holding Rex's leash, "You'll let me know if Max is back, right?"

"I will! Don't worry!" Ben grins and gives me a thumbs-up.

Despite my nerves, Stacy works her charm, and before I know it, I'm booked for a full two-hour hot stone massage, facial, and aromatherapy. If it were up to me, I'd sit and worry, but Stacy's in charge now.

So, I go with it.

The dim lighting, gentle sounds of nature, even the fake waterfall in the spa lobby all soothe me.

The next two hours blur between calm and chaos. My mind flips every minute or two—from telling myself I deserve this break, to feeling guilty that Jasper's killer is still out there.

It's a battle I can't seem to win.

But at least my aching back relaxes.

I feel refreshed, if only a little.

When we leave, no messages from Ben or Cole say Max is back.

"See?" Stacy beams over my shoulder, glowing from the treatments. "Told you he wouldn't be back this soon."

"Or maybe he won't come back at all," I mutter, uneasy.

"Want to bet?" Stacy challenges, raising an eyebrow. "Men like The Ace follow money. And this city doesn't have casinos—so he'll be back."

I eye her suspiciously. "When did you research that?"

"At the spa," she admits casually. "Figured giving you a reason not to worry would help."

"Stacy," I say, my heart swelling, "that's so sweet."

"Don't get too touched—I did it for my boyfriend. Otherwise, you'd be pestering him until Max shows up," she teases.

I laugh. "Yeah, right."

"Believe what you want. Just telling the truth." She starts walking away, and I follow. "How about a smoothie?"

"Perfect for the weather," I say, bracing for a slow afternoon.

Then my phone pings.

Relaxation evaporates.

Ben's message: Reception just told me Max is here. I'm on my way.

I freeze, staring at the screen like it's a lifeline. "Um, Stace, maybe you get that smoothie alone."

"What?" Stacy spins, dark hair flowing.

I say, "Max's back. Reception area. I should—"

"Go!" Stacy yells, hands motioning urgently.

"See you later!" I sprint past her, racing down hallways and stairs, desperate to see Max myself.

Even knowing he's back doesn't calm me. Too many questions hammer at my skull, begging for answers.

I spot Ben jogging down the grand stairs with Rex, just steps from the reception, where Max is talking to the receptionist.

"Thanks for holding Rex," I say, grabbing his leash and descending carefully but quickly.

A VIP taps Ben halfway down the stairs. "Captain Anderson!"

I barely glance as Ben nods at me, urging me to go on. "Mr. Ludwig..."

Refusing to miss meeting The Ace in person, Rex and I push forward. Max edges closer with each step.

A few feet away, I hear Max ask, "Can you at least tell me if Jasper Thorne is still on the ship? I'm worried about him."

As if he knows nothing.

The receptionist turns to me expectantly. "Miss Dela Cruz, I heard you were looking for Mr. Parrish."

Max slowly turns. His face drains of color for reasons I don't understand.

Breathless, I step closer. "Mr. Parrish—"

Before I can say more, he bolts, almost tripping as he rushes down the hallway, trying to escape.

But why?

No time to wonder.

I have to chase him—no matter what, no matter why.

Chapter 20

Max Parrish bolts away from me like his life depends on it, sneakers scraping hard against the polished floor. He risks a glance over his shoulder and spots me and Rex closing in fast.

"Mr. Parrish!" I call sharply, determination burning through my voice.

The twisting hallways stretch out ahead of him. He runs past staterooms and crew areas, eyes locked straight forward like nothing else matters.

This isn't how I imagined we'd meet. The thought flashes through my mind as I chase after him. His reputation doesn't match this—Max Parrish, the composed professional, running like a scared kid. Yet here he is, sprinting down corridors like escape is his only option.

Why is he running? I don't have a clue.

"Mr. Parrish! Stop! I just want to talk," I call again, but the ship's engine hum and ocean waves swallow my voice.

Then Rex lunges forward with a low growl, tenacious as ever. I watch as Rex darts past me, eyes locked on Max. With a quick nip, Rex playfully bites the edge of Max's pant leg—enough to make him stumble and fall forward.

I seize the moment to close the distance.

Max scrambles backward into a sitting position, suddenly smaller and more vulnerable, only to freeze as Rex growls again.

"It's alright, buddy," I say softly, calming Rex. Then I turn to Max.

His eyes meet mine, pupils wide with fear. He blurts out, "Okay! I'm sorry! Please! I don't want to get in trouble!"

I blink, slightly thrown off. Is this him confessing to Jasper's murder? Or is it something else entirely?

Before I can ask, I offer my hand. "Get up first, okay? Then we'll talk."

This time, Max doesn't resist. I lead him toward the conference room-turned-interrogation space. Ben, Cole, Stacy, and Julia are already waiting.

Max's nervous eyes scan the cramped room filled with stiff, expectant faces. Behind him, Rex growls low and steady. Max knows better than to refuse the safer option: going inside.

He sinks into an empty chair while the others wait in tense silence. Ben's face is tight with stress. Cole's jaw clenched so hard I can almost hear it grind. Stacy's lips press into a hard line, and Julia clutches her notebook like a lifeline.

I sit across from Max and press the recorder button on the table.

We've wasted enough time. I dive straight in. "Mr. Parrish, my name's Rose Dela Cruz. I'm the cruise director. Is there something you want to tell us?"

Max mumbles, hesitant. "No...?"

I press. "Then why did you run from me earlier?"

His gaze flickers, fingers nervously massaging one another. "Why were you chasing me?" he shoots back, voice a mix of confusion and anxiety.

"Because you ran first," I say, voice firm. "Like you'd been caught."

Max's eyes dart around the room full of impatient faces. For a moment, he looks like he wants to keep playing it smart. Then he sighs, defeated. "I... I thought you were after me because of the first poker tournament."

"The tournament?" I echo, eyebrows raised. "Why would I be?"

He hesitates. "Because... I'm a card shark, okay? I figured maybe you knew. Maybe my partner threw me under the bus. No wonder he's been hiding from me."

Ben leans forward. "Your partner? Jasper Thorne?"

Max leans back, a ghost of relief flickering across his face. "See? He told you, didn't he?"

Ben and I exchange a quick glance—apologetic but firm. I meet Max's eyes again. "Jasper couldn't have told us anything, Mr. Parrish."

Max raises an eyebrow, as if mocking me. "Couldn't? Not wouldn't?"

Cole cuts in, calm but direct. "Jasper's dead, Mr. Parrish. He died three days ago—right after the tournament."

Max blinks, like the words haven't sunk in. Then a hollow chuckle escapes. "Yeah, right. The guy wouldn't die that easily."

"But he did," I say, face serious. Max sees the truth there.

His eyes widen. "Wait... are you serious?"

My gut tells me he's innocent, and maybe Max believes it too.

He shudders, clutching his stomach like nausea might hit at any moment. "Oh, Jesus..."

Julia rushes over with a water bottle. Max stares at it a moment before taking a sloppy sip.

I break the silence. "You really had no idea, did you?"

"That Jasper's dead?" Max swallows hard. "I spent the last three days looking for him! I was worried!"

Stacy narrows her eyes. "Him? Or the money?"

Max opens his mouth, closes it, then tries again. "I'd be a hypocrite to say no to the money. He and I—we work together on these tournaments. I help him win, and he pays me a cut."

I knew it, but now's not the time to congratulate myself. Jasper's killer is still out there.

Max goes on, "But he's stopped answering my calls. I thought maybe he got caught cheating, or was hiding somewhere. Maybe even hiding from me because I'd been named. That's why I ran."

I let out a slow breath. "Alright. If it wasn't you who killed Jasper, then who?"

For the first time, Max's face lights up. "The high rollers. They hate Jasper. They were pissed when he won the first game."

"We're looking into them, too," I admit, trusting him just a bit. "But no proof yet. They don't exactly open up to outsiders."

Max leans forward, eyes bright. "Exactly. They only trust their own."

"Meaning?" Stacy crosses her arms, waiting.

"Meaning... they might tell something to someone within their circle." Max's brain races, ideas pouring out. "If you let me, I can help you find Jasper's killer."

Admittedly, I'm intrigued.

I lean forward, eyes locked on him. "And how exactly can you help us?"

"It's simple," Max says with confidence. "We infiltrate their group by putting a new but impressive poker player in tonight's tournament. That'll grab their attention."

I glance around the room. None of us knows poker well enough to win a tournament. Well, Ben might—but he's the captain; everyone would recognize him instantly. So who?

My gaze lands on Max. "So, you're saying we send you into the tournament?"

"What? No!" Max's reaction catches me off guard. He shakes his head. "Look, I may be a card shark, but I'm the kind who works behind the scenes. I can't sit down in front of those players without blowing my cover. I'm too nervous!"

There's a crack in his voice that makes me wonder if his reputation has been exaggerated. How can a nervous guy like Max be The Ace? Maybe he's more urban legend than reality—and a bit disappointing.

Cole cuts in. "If it's not you, then who? Most of us here would be recognized immediately by those high rollers."

"Most of you," Max agrees, nodding. "But some won't be—which ones?"

Four pairs of eyes immediately turn to Stacy. She's the only one here who isn't a crew member of The Midnight Tide. Plus, she has that effortless elegance and poise of someone from the high-stakes poker world.

Right now, Stacy looks like the perfect fit.

Max agrees. "I was betting on her, too. It'd be easier to get those guys talking with a pretty face."

Stacy doesn't even blink at the compliment—she's heard it a hundred times before. Instead, she huffs. "This would've been a good idea if I actually knew how to play poker."

"You don't have to know the game," Max insists. "Like Jasper, you just need an earpiece and a good bluff. How well can you act?"

Stacy shrugs. "Not well."

I squint at her. "Didn't you join the theater in high school? I thought you were pretty good."

"That was one time," Stacy shoots back. "And I was forced into it."

"But you still did great," I say with a smile. "Think you can bluff? Honestly, I don't see anyone else pulling it off but you."

Stacy holds my gaze for a few seconds, like she's daring me to be serious. Then she sighs, conceding. "Fine. But how does this plan work?"

Max jumps in, excitement sparking in his eyes. "We put you in the tournament, impress the high rollers, invite them for drinks afterward, and get them talking about Jasper."

Stacy's eyes widen, nervousness flickering across her face—but then she straightens up and says, "Sounds simple enough. You did say I'd get an earpiece, right?"

"Absolutely," Max nods. "I'll do all the playing. Don't worry."

Chapter 21

I just don't think this is a good idea, Cole says as I help Stacy put on her gold necklace—her initial shining softly against her skin.

Julia, who's been eyeing Stacy's dress—a strapless, floor-length dusty rose gown with a sleek, streamlined bodice—smirks at Cole. "You'd think that, considering Stacy's going to be surrounded by all those gentlemen looking like that!"

Cole's cheeks flush a little, and Stacy smiles at him through the mirror's reflection. He replies defensively, "I just mean those men could be dangerous. Who knows?"

"That's why we'll be right behind Stacy the whole time." I finish fastening the necklace, its delicate gold perfectly matching her dress. Now, Stacy really looks the part—a wealthy woman ready for a casual night—or maybe not so casual—at the casino.

Stacy steps toward Cole, takes his hand. "I'll be fine. You're going to watch after me, right?"

"Of course." His smile is small but real, his worries melting away at her touch.

Before the moment can get any more lovey-dovey, there's a knock at the door. Julia hurries over and opens it. Max stands there, an excited grin lighting up his face, dressed in a crisp shirt.

"Hello there."

"You clean up nice," I say as he steps inside.

Max grins. "I have to look like I at least belong in the casino."

"How are you even going to make me win? I don't know a thing about poker," Stacy admits, unfazed by her lack of gambling skills.

Max pulls a translucent earpiece from his shirt pocket and hands it to Stacy. "Just listen to every word I say. I'll make sure you win tonight's tournament."

And that's exactly what he does.

After Stacy charms her fellow players—including Chase and Joe—the tournament kicks off.

Max moves around the poker table like he's reading everyone's cards, quietly deciding Stacy's next move. With her hair tucked behind one ear, no one notices the earpiece.

Just like Jasper last time.

At first, Max plays it slow so the other men won't get suspicious of this new player. But as the game goes on, Stacy starts to show off her skills and luck—both thanks to Max. As long as the men don't know that, we're safe.

Cole, Julia, and I watch from the sidelines. Someone calls, someone folds, someone goes all in. Eventually, Stacy matches the stakes. And before anyone realizes what's happening, Stacy wins.

Maybe Max is right. When the pretty girl wins, all the boys at the table seem impressed. Not one accuses her of cheating—even though she is.

After brief congratulations, the men rise with satisfied smiles. A few hand Stacy their calling cards and ask for hers. Cole visibly tenses. Thankfully, Stacy's good at brushing off unwanted attention.

She lingers just behind as the players disperse, pretending to touch up her lipstick before nodding at me.

It's showtime—the real showtime.

As the others disappear, Stacy approaches Chase and Joe. She taps one on the shoulder. "Hey, I was wondering if we could get some drinks."

Chase smirks—the kind of smirk that makes Cole clench his fists. "Does that mean you have nowhere else to be?"

"Oh, my sister's on a date somewhere on the ship," Stacy lies smoothly. "I have no one to drink with until then. So, what do you say?"

Chase doesn't even check with Joe. He steps aside, giving Stacy space. "After you."

Stacy leads them to the poolside bar on the upper deck, just like we planned. As Chase and Joe trail behind, Cole and I follow a few steps back. Meanwhile, Max and Julia head to the bridge with Ben to record Stacy's conversation with the suspects.

"How're you holding up?" I gently tap Cole's back. He stiffens at my touch.

Before he answers, I already know. "I'd be glad to take her away from here already."

"Just a few more minutes, okay?" I try to reassure him. "Once we get what we need, we'll get her out—fast."

Cole breathes in deeply. "Of course."

The salt breeze hits my face; the wind tosses my hair and nips cold air into my lungs.

At this hour, the poolside bar buzzes with life. Passengers chat and laugh over flavored drinks while servers move swiftly between tables.

Cole and I slip quietly to a table behind the group. We keep our heads low so neither Chase nor Joe notices us.

Chase orders drinks while Stacy and Joe sit awkwardly; Joe clearly isn't as interested in Stacy as Chase is. Chase returns quickly with a tray of three different drinks. He sits a little too close to Stacy. She hides her discomfort behind a smile and gets straight to the point.

The charade must be wearing on her.

"So," Stacy begins, stirring her olive on a toothpick into her dirty martini, "any of you friends with that lucky player? From the first tournament—Jasper Thorne, wasn't it?"

Chase groans, not even bothering to hide his dislike for Jasper. "I wonder why everyone's obsessed with that guy—Jasper this, Jasper that. The guy's a cheater, not lucky."

"Oh? Sounds like you and him got beef," Stacy says, raising her eyebrows in interest.

Joe speaks this time. "We wouldn't call it beef; Jasper's just... annoying, to say the least."

"Well, you must be glad he wasn't in the tournament," Stacy presses.

"Absolutely!" Chase chuckles. "But I'd love to crush him under my thumb one of these days."

Joe takes a sip of his gin and tonic, muttering, "I already did."

Chase and Joe exchange a knowing look, breaking into smiles, snorts, even laughter.

Though I'm just a few feet away, I hear Joe clearly—even over the wind and the groaning ship. Goosebumps crawl up my arms.

Stacy, just as appalled, tries to get them to explain. "What's that supposed to mean? You've beaten him at poker before?"

Joe leans in, voice dripping arrogance. "Let's just say I beat him, alright."

For the first time, Joe sounds as arrogant as Chase—maybe even more. His cryptic words make him feel like a devil in disguise.

Could it be Joe who walked up to Jasper's suite and strangled him to death? If not poker, did he at least beat Jasper at life?

"Anyhow," Chase says, shifting the subject, "let's not talk about that jerk. Let's talk about you, Stacy. So, where are you from?"

This is where I want to get Stacy out of here, but then I notice Joe's posture shift. His back stiffens as his gaze darts toward the other side of the deck.

I follow his line of sight and spot a familiar figure standing by the railings, smoking and staring out into the dark ocean.

It's Benson.

Benson breaks his gaze from the siren call of the waves and locks eyes with Joe. At that exact moment, Joe shoves his chair back and nudges Chase. "We should go."

"What? Why?" Chase complains, clearly confused.

Unlike Joe, Chase seems oblivious to whoever else might be around. Still, Joe grabs him by the arm. "Didn't I tell you I've got an important meeting tonight? Let's move."

"Yeah, but that's you..." Chase protests, frowning.

Right then, Stacy interrupts. "Please, don't let me keep your other company waiting. I should head inside, too."

Chase's disappointment deepens, the lines on his face tightening. "But..."

Stacy stands, grabs her purse, and heads for the exit. "Nice meeting you both."

Immediately, Cole rises and follows Stacy off the deck.

I stay behind, watching Joe exchange one last look with Benson. They nod to each other before Joe leaves.

The three of them—or maybe just Joe and Benson—seem to be silently stalking one another in a tense, unspoken agreement.

It makes me wonder what that strange, guarded exchange means.

Am I just grasping at straws here, or are Joe and Benson already colluding about something dark?

Like Jasper's death, maybe?

Chapter 22

No matter the hour, the bridge hums with quiet purpose. Officers move with steady focus, their electronics glowing softly against the darkness of the ocean beyond. The sea stretches out, seamless and black, broken only by distant winks of fishing boats somewhere far off.

As I step inside, the group is already gathered around the center table. Ben stands in the middle, commanding attention as always in his uniform. Cole sits beside Stacy, who looks drained after a long night of acting. Julia has her notebook open, ready. Rex wags his tail at me, happy to see a familiar face. Max pads around the room, taking in the space like he's on a grand tour of The Midnight Tide.

I crouch to greet Rex before turning to Stacy. "Good job tonight, Stace."

She rolls her eyes, playful. "Tell me about it."

"No, seriously," Julia adds, silver headband glinting under the bridge lights. "You were convincing. Like this isn't your first time at poker."

Stacy points to her earpiece, now resting on the table. "All thanks to Max."

Max spins around from the screen he's been studying. "So, I still get a payout, right?"

I glare. "You're lucky we're not banning you from The Midnight Tide altogether."

He raises his hands, surrendering. "Hey, at least I tried."

Ben's voice cuts in, steady and calm. "So, what's our next move?"

Before I can answer, Stacy jumps in. "We're on the right track. Chase Ford and Joe Booker gave us enough to be suspicious. Joe said something about beating Jasper—not at poker, obviously—so could that be a subtle confession?"

"I heard it too," I say. "Thought the same thing. But it's too vague. We need concrete evidence. Something undeniable."

Cole leans forward. "Like what?"

I pause. "Like... Jasper's money bag."

Max's face lights up, but I shoot him a warning look before he can get any ideas.

"It's the best proof we can get," I say firmly. "I'm certain the money bag's still on the ship. None of our suspects left with it earlier."

Ben nods in agreement. "Then let's search their rooms."

Julia raises her hand slowly, like a student unsure if she should speak. "Wouldn't they just deny us access? If they're involved with Jasper's murder, they'd probably want us to stay out of their private spaces."

"Not with probable cause," Ben says confidently. We've used this tactic before and it's worked. No doubt it'll work again.

Julia's curiosity wins over. "And what would the probable cause be?"

Ben thinks for a moment. "We say Stacy lost something valuable during the tournament—a diamond ring, maybe. Then we take it from there."

"That could work..." Cole hesitates, thinking through the risks. "But that excuse only applies to the poker players like Chase and Joe. What about Benson?"

"He's close with Joe," I say, remembering the strange encounter earlier. "I think there's more there—maybe a secret. I saw them at the bar. When Benson showed up, Joe jumped up. Not sure if Chase noticed or not, but something's definitely going on."

"Can we use that to get into Benson's room?" Cole asks.

"We have to try," I say, though my voice betrays some doubt.

Even with our authority, we have to respect that these suspects are passengers. They can refuse us, accuse us of invading their privacy.

It's just another obstacle standing between us and justice for Jasper.

Ben's voice cuts through the thoughts. "We make this the first priority tomorrow morning. Make it urgent."

We all nod, silence settling over the room except for the steady beeping of the navigation system and the ship cutting through the ocean.

"Just one more thing," Cole says softly. "Did anyone notice the... whispers in the casino?"

"Whispers?" Stacy turns to him, curious. She'd been too busy with the tournament to catch anything like that. "What do you mean?"

I'm surprised Cole noticed anything besides Stacy. I was too focused on her all night, making sure none of those poker guys got too close.

Cole's expression darkens. "The casino managers and dealers at other tables—they're talking privately more than usual. Almost like they're planning something."

"Or maybe we're just paranoid?" Max pipes up, earning five pairs of eyes glaring at him. He backtracks. "I just mean... with Jasper's death, we're all on edge, suspicious."

Cole shrugs off Max's comment. "Maybe. But doesn't it strike you as odd how often dealers 'check in' with the manager?"

"How often?" I ask, feeling guilty I didn't notice.

"Enough times for me to notice," Cole says.

I glance at Ben, searching for reassurance. He nods slightly.

"You know what? Let's look into that, too," I say. "Maybe Jude knows more than he lets on."

Julia frowns. "But he seems trustworthy."

"Seems trustworthy doesn't mean he is," I remind her, learning from hard experience.

Julia can only nod, holding back a sigh.

Ben stands. "That's our two orders of business for tomorrow. For now, let's call it a night."

I grin. "Aye, aye, captain."

The eastern horizon awakens The Midnight Tide, and the diamond-like shimmer of the sun on the water welcomes the new day. I stretch awake, bleary-eyed but eager. Ready. Nervous.

Rex stretches after stepping out of his bed, his way of saying it's time to start another day of solving mysteries.

I get out of bed, preparing Rex's food first before showering, dressing, and stepping into the hallway. There, I run into Julia—bright in her red polka-dot dress, matching earrings, and Mary Janes.

"Good morning, Mrs. Claus," I tease.

Julia rolls her eyes, eyeing my dull navy suit jacket and pants. "Good morning, boring blue lady." Her face softens as Rex appears behind me. "And you too, little buddy."

Rex puts on a show, hopping and spinning in circles before Julia.

"Looks like you're ready to sniff out clues, huh?" she says.

"When is he not?" I reply with a proud smile.

Julia turns to me. "Off to find Jasper's money bag?"

Ben and I will get started on the script for that. We might have to check every player's room—suspects or not—so Chase and Joe won't suspect we're onto them.

"How about me?" Julia's eyes sparkle with excitement.

We walk toward our shared office as I say, "You and Cole can look into Jude and any other shady casino dealings. Stacy's stepping away from the scenes for now. We don't want a target on her back."

"Sounds great!" Julia agrees enthusiastically.

For the first hour, Julia and I huddle in our office, double-checking today's schedule: a 10 a.m. marine biology lecture for kids at the library, four movie screenings at the cinema, and a 7 p.m. classical band show in the dining hall.

With the day mostly quiet, Julia can easily check in on events while we focus on the investigation.

I push the schedule aside and meet Ben at the suites, where most poker players' rooms are.

Ben smiles when he sees me and Rex. "Slept well last night?"

"Good enough," I admit. I tossed and turned for hours. Rex had to cuddle me to stop me from getting tangled in the sheets. "You?"

"Would've slept better with you beside me." Ben smirks.

I snort. "Yeah, right. Ready to ruin some people's mornings by going through their stuff?"

"Part of the job." Ben shrugs, eyes on the first door on our left. It's not Chase, Joe, or Benson's room, but checking other rooms is necessary to make our story convincing.

Ben nods and presses the doorbell.

"Hi, good morning. Captain Ben Anderson here. Sorry to interrupt so early, but we're looking for a missing ring from last night's tournament. We think it was lost or stolen. May we search your room?" he asks.

We're met with resistance—these wealthy players don't appreciate being accused, especially when they can buy diamond rings themselves.

But we're not really looking for Stacy's missing ring.

Still, the tension hangs heavy as we open drawers, closets, suitcases, check under beds, chairs, and behind bathroom cabinets. Nightstands creak, clothes rustle, zippers slide. Players click tongues, sigh, mumble disappointments.

Even Rex puts on a show, sniffing meticulously.

We work our way through rooms until we reach Chase and Joe's floor—their rooms side by side.

We start with Joe's suite, hoping he's cooperative.

Ben rings, Joe opens the door, rubbing his eyes. "Yes?"

"Mr. Booker," Ben says with a friendly smile. "Sorry to wake you. We need your cooperation."

Ben explains Stacy lost a diamond ring during the tournament and fears it was stolen by a player or their acquaintance—the last part setting us up to search Benson's room next.

Joe hesitates briefly, then steps aside. "Please, come in."

His confidence makes me doubt his involvement, though the pit in my stomach won't ease. I tug Rex inside.

We search the usual spots: beside, behind, and under the bed; closet; bathroom cabinets.

Rex roams, sniffing for clues, but finds nothing.

Ben and I pretend to check coat pockets and sock drawers—more convincing.

Minutes later, we thank Joe and step out.

Before the door closes, I ask, "That other poker guy—Benson Wolf—you're friends, right?"

I expect surprise, but Joe barely reacts, wiggling his nose. "We've played tournaments together, that's all."

"But you met last night, didn't you? I thought I saw you while making rounds," I lie—I wasn't making rounds; I was watching.

Joe shrugs. "We bought whisky and drank in his suite. Problem?"

"Nope. Just figured we'd pay him a visit too," I say.

Joe's lips curl into a smug smile. "You think a billionaire like him would steal a diamond ring?"

"Oh, you never know," I say, backing away.

Joe keeps his door open, eyes on us as we cross the hall to Chase's room.

He opens, scowling. "What's this early morning nonsense?"

"Don't resist," Joe calls from down the hall. "Just go with it."

"Why?" Chase eyes us skeptically.

"That girl you were hitting on last night—she lost a diamond ring," Joe explains with disbelief.

Chase narrows his eyes. "She said I took it?"

"No, Mr. Ford," I say firmly this time. "We're just checking all the players' rooms to confirm nothing's been stolen."

Chase lets out a mirthless laugh. "What a ton of—"

"Just go with it," Joe cuts in again, voice steady. "You didn't steal it, did you?"

Chase shakes his head, then steps aside, probably to trash-talk us with Joe. He gestures weakly toward the door. "Have at it."

Ignoring the judgment, Ben, Rex, and I enter the room and begin the search—both for the money bag and the missing ring that doesn't exist. Like Joe's room, Chase's is a snapshot of a messy vacation—clothes everywhere, half-read paperbacks scattered, toiletries piled on the bathroom sink, and a suitcase only half tucked into the closet.

After dealing with two of our main suspects, we finally arrive at Benson's suite. Nearby, Jasper's now-empty room looms unsettlingly close.

As we approach, Benson is just about to leave. "Can I help you?"

Once again, Ben explains Stacy's lost diamond ring and Benson's connection to Joe, suggesting the ring might be in Benson's suite. Benson doesn't question us; instead, he lets us in, looking impatient as he picks up a magazine I'm sure he won't read.

Rex immediately gets to work, sniffing every inch of Benson's unnervingly pristine bedroom. Even the duvet is folded perfectly at the edges. Ben moves deliberately through the room, eyes sharp on Benson as he inspects the obvious hiding spots. I do the same.

Then Rex growls low and urgent at the bedside drawer. It's the kind of growl that demands attention.

Rex stands on his hind legs and paws at the drawer's door.

I don't hesitate. It's the first reaction Rex's had all morning—I know he's onto something.

Trusting Rex, I move closer. Rex backs down as I pull the drawer open. Behind me, Ben peers over my shoulder, curious about what's causing Rex's alarm.

The drawer creaks quietly as it slides open. Inside, I see a few items—a leather wallet, a luxury watch, a pamphlet for The Midnight Tide—and then something that makes my breath hitch.

"Is that...?" Ben trails off, eyes fixed on the object.

I manage to say it for him. "...a gold chip."

The same one Jasper had over his eyes when we found his body.

The realization dawns slowly, suffocating me.

Why does Benson have the same thing?

Chapter 23

Benson Wolf sits across from me in the conference room. Between us on the table lie a running recorder and the gold chip we found tucked in his drawer.

The ship's hum and vibrations feel louder than usual in the heavy silence—the kind of silence that forms when you're hunting for the right words to ask—or accuse—someone.

"Why am I here again?" Benson asks, arms crossed, posture defensive.

Ben watches everything from the corner, while Rex sits upright beside me, every muscle alert.

My eyes settle on the gold chip. "We found this chip in your nightstand drawer, Mr. Wolf."

"I thought you were looking for a diamond ring," Benson replies, his calm face betraying no worry or guilt about the same object left poetically over Jasper's dead body.

That chip—innocent as it looks—is enough to pull me back to the night of Jasper's murder. How unnerving it was to find something like this over a dead man, then discover something similar in someone's drawer.

"We were," I say after a beat, my mind spinning a parallel monologue apart from this conversation. "But this—this piques our interest."

"How so? You think I stole it from the casino or something?" Benson sounds casual, like he has no clue why this chip matters.

Leaning against the wall, Ben cuts in, "You couldn't have stolen it from our casino, Mr. Wolf. We don't use gold chips."

I add, "Which leads us to wonder—where did you get this in the first place?"

A small, hesitant smile tugs at Benson's lips. "Is this some kind of joke?"

I keep my face neutral. "Does it look like we're joking?"

"I don't know. You tell me." Benson tightens his arms across his chest—like he's cold... or bracing himself.

Ben steps forward. "What do you mean by that?"

Benson chuckles, voice light but sharp. "I got this gold chip as an invitation to the tournament here on the ship. Came in the mail a few days before the cruise. So why are you acting like you don't know about it?"

I glance at Ben. Our shared ignorance on this? It only confirms one thing: this chip is not supposed to exist. Not on our watch. Not without our knowledge. And if Benson's telling the truth—then why don't the other players have gold chips? We searched their belongings, too.

Did we miss theirs? Did they not bring it? Or is Benson spinning a story to throw us off?

I turn back to Benson. "That's impossible, Mr. Wolf. We didn't send out invitations. Players have to sign up for the tournament."

"Well, what do you want me to say?" Benson shrugs, patience thinning but no real distress showing. "I got it in the mail. Whether you knew about it or not, I don't see the big deal."

My jaw tightens. "It is a big deal, Mr. Wolf. Especially since we found these same chips on... Jasper Thorne."

"On Jasper?" Benson echoes, confused.

Ben exhales. "Over his eyes, to be precise."

Benson's gaze flicks between us. "I don't know where you're going with this, but maybe you should call Jasper here, too. We can all talk about these gold chips."

"You don't understand, Mr. Wolf." I fix him with a steady look. "We can't call Jasper here to explain why he has the same chips as you... because we found his over his eyes—after he... died."

My voice catches; I almost choke on the words.

For a moment, Benson looks lost. His eyes narrow, head tilts, then he exhales deeply. "He's dead? Jasper's dead?"

His shock looks real—creased brows, tight frown, tense shoulders. I watch the change, noting only surprise at the news.

"Unfortunately, we believe Jasper was murdered," I say, swallowing hard as my throat constricts.

"So that's why he disappeared." Benson sneers, a chillingly casual response to a murder.

I glare at him. He shrugs and says, "Look, I told you—I followed Jasper here to get my money back, but I didn't kill him. I thought your questions and elaborate setups were strange, but now it makes sense. If you think I'm a murderer, let me ease your mind—I'm not. I want my money back more than a dead body on my hands."

Despite his attempt to reassure us, I get mixed feelings. His shock feels off-kilter, too casual for such heavy news. It's like he's showing me what I want—but too laidback, too cool for murder.

How can anyone sound this unbothered after hearing that? How does his surprise fade so fast? How does he treat murder like weather?

Is he uninvolved? Or involved but confident he can get away with it?

My mind spins with the endless questions.

Sensing my tension, Ben steps in. "We'd appreciate it if you don't tell anyone about Mr. Thorne's death. We don't want to panic the passengers."

"So you believe me when I say I didn't kill Jasper?" Benson asks.

"Let's just say we're letting you off for now," Ben answers firmly. "But we're watching you."

"That almost sounds like a threat." Benson stands, pulling his chair back. "Now, can I go?"

Ben nods, not waiting for me. My head swims with thoughts as Benson leaves.

Ben checks on me. "Tough conversation?"

I breathe deep, grounding myself with the ship's steady rhythm—the ocean slapping the hull a reminder of where I am. "I just don't know what to make of Benson."

"Don't get caught up in feelings, Rose." Ben squeezes my shoulder. "Let's follow the evidence."

My eyes drop back to the gold chip sitting on the table. Of course.

So that's exactly what Ben and I do next—we follow the evidence.

After clearing my head of swirling doubts, Ben, Rex, and I head to the casino, where Cole and Julia have been keeping watch all morning.

The room is bright with sunlight pouring through tall windows, mixed with the soft blue glow from the slot machines. Cole and Julia patrol with sharp eyes and tight lips, their focus razor-thin.

Jude, used to our presence, acts as normal as ever—unaware we're here for him this time.

"Hey." I catch Cole's eye as I close the distance.

He stops pacing; Julia's just behind him. "You took your time," Cole says, casual but alert.

I keep my voice low. "Guess what we found and who we talked to."

Cole glances between me and Ben. "What and who?"

Julia's attention snaps fully to us.

Ben frowns. "A gold chip—like the one found over Jasper's eyes. We found it in Benson Wolf's room."

Cole's eyes widen. Groundbreaking, to say the least. "So? Does this mean he...?"

He trails off, but we know what he means.

"We don't know what it means yet," I answer. "Especially since Benson has an... interesting explanation for having it."

Julia leans in, curious. "Which is?"

"An unauthorized invitation," I say slowly, still wrapping my head around Benson's words. "Sent from this casino."

Just then, Jude appears—prim and proper as ever. "Captain Anderson, Miss Dela Cruz. Another busy morning? Anything I can help with?"

Ben gives me a quick nod. No time for small talk. Justice needs to happen, and fast.

"I'm glad you asked, Jude." I pull the gold chip from my pocket and hold it up. "We're hoping you can tell us where this came from."

Jude barely reacts. Innocent, almost. "Uh... I thought we made it clear we don't have gold chips in this casino."

"We did," I say, my expression souring. "Yet a passenger claims this was sent as an invitation to the poker tournament."

Jude's composure cracks just slightly; he clears his throat nervously. "I... I don't think that's possible, Miss Dela Cruz. Players have to sign up personally."

"That's what we thought," Ben cuts in, voice firm. "Which makes it strange that a passenger would make such a specific claim without any truth."

"Well..." Jude chuckles nervously. "I don't know what to tell you, Captain. It's a specific claim, yes, but one I have no knowledge of."

I hold Jude's gaze long enough to unsettle him. "Is that true?"

"Of course." His smile is stiff. "I have no reason to lie."

Though Jude seems composed, Rex's sudden bark shatters the moment, slicing through the casino's ambient noise.

All eyes snap to Rex, who bolts deeper into the casino, yanking his leash from my hand.

"Rex!" I call after him, heart racing as he charges toward the back rooms with clear purpose.

I follow without hesitation—better to keep him close than have him disturb passengers.

Four sets of footsteps scramble behind us, but my eyes stay locked on Rex. He heads straight for a door left slightly ajar—the manager's office, according to the sign.

"Hold up!" Jude shouts behind me, but Rex and I are already inside.

Rex stands on his hind legs, paws scrabbling at the drawer on Jude's desk. He looks at me with those beady eyes that scream *something's here*.

Ignoring Jude's protests as he rushes in, I pull open the drawer with intention.

By the time Jude and the others enter, I'm staring wide-eyed at what's inside.

Scattered across the drawer are several gold chips, half-hidden beneath a messy stack of papers.

Anyone with functioning eyes can see they're the same gold chips we found over Jasper's eyes—and in Benson's room.

But why are they here?

And the bigger question—

Has Jude been playing us all along?

Chapter 24

"No gold chips in the casino, huh?" I say aloud, mostly to myself, as I pick up one of the gold chips from Jude's drawers. The familiar weight and gleam mock me—like the answers I've been chasing have been hiding in plain sight all along.

Jude's so-called attentiveness? Turns out he was just checking if we'd caught on.

Well, now he has. The blood rushing down his face drains the color from his skin. Jude stammers, "I... I can explain."

Behind him, Cole and Julia block the doorway like sentinels. Then Ben looms over Jude, his expression carved from betrayal and fury.

The porthole beside Jude's desk frames a calm sea—the blues melting into an endless horizon. But there's no calm in this room. I can feel my anger bubbling just beneath the surface.

I never fully trusted Jude, but I didn't expect this. Now the tension between us is so thick, it feels like you could cut it with a knife.

"You better have a damn good explanation," Ben says, voice low and grim.

Jude shuffles back a step, scanning the room for a friendly face—finding none. He finally looks at me. "Miss Dela

Cruz, please believe me when I say those gold chips don't mean trouble."

"Believe you?" I echo, bitterness prickling my tongue. "I asked you about these chips more than once. You lied every single time."

"Only because I—"

"What are they for?" Ben cuts in sharply. Respect died the moment Jude's lies surfaced.

Jude's gaze drops to the floor. If he's thinking up another lie, I hope we catch it fast. Then his voice squeaks out, "It's an exclusive invitation to a private poker tournament in the VIP rooms."

His apologetic tone barely masks the truth. My breath catches. "You mean an unauthorized private tournament."

"In layman's terms, yes," Jude admits, refusing to meet my eyes.

A heavy silence falls. Our first time running a casino aboard The Midnight Tide has backfired spectacularly.

Ben runs a frustrated hand down his face. "And you were the mastermind behind this? For what? Bigger payouts?"

Jude's shame is obvious now. "A few dealers and I came up with the idea. We figured personal invites to high-stakes players would boost... income. These players care about exclusivity more than commercial tournaments."

"And without cruise management's knowledge, you'd pocket the fees—at a premium," Julia adds, her time researching the casino showing.

Jude nods slowly, shrinking under our scrutiny like a man caught on a sinking ship.

My knees weaken. I clutch the edge of the desk to steady myself. The ship's rocking suddenly feels sharper, the ocean below unsteady beneath me. The thought of an underground poker ring operating under my watch churns my stomach.

Ben's jaw tightens, barely containing his anger.

Between this and Jasper's death... I'm overwhelmed. But Jasper's life comes first.

I force myself to speak. "Did Jasper Thorne get an invite?"

Jude shakes his head. "No. He's got a bad rep in the poker world. We left him off to avoid upsetting other VIP players."

So those gold chips over Jasper's eyes? Not his.

Despite feeling vulnerable standing before this liar, I decide to be honest. "Jasper had gold chips in his room when we found him after the first tournament..."

"Found him?" Jude's eyes finally meet mine.

"Yes," I say, bile rising with the words as always. "We found him dead that night, Jude."

His eyes widen, disbelief etched across his face. "What? You mean Mr. Thorne is...?"

"Dead," Cole cuts in firmly—cold but precise. "That's why it's critical we know where those gold chips came from. Because of you, we wasted days chasing what those chips meant to Jasper's death."

"It means nothing!" Jude blurts, panic creeping in. "I swear. We ran the other tournament, but those gold chips? Just invitations. Nothing more!"

"It's not nothing anymore, Jude," I bite out. The casino's hum and ship's drone drown out my own breath—if I'm even breathing. "Our biggest clue to Jasper's killer is those gold chips left over his eyes—some kind of message. Maybe a sick 'sending off.' Until we know who left them, we don't know who killed Jasper."

Jude pales further. Sweat beads at his forehead; his lips dry. "Please, you have to understand. I only sent the chips as invites. I don't know anything about Mr. Thorne's... murder."

"How can we trust you at this point?" Ben fires the question like a bullet.

"I... I..." Jude stammers, eyes darting like an escape hatch might open on the walls. Then, a spark. "I can give you the VIP invite list to prove I'm innocent!"

For the first time since discovering Jude's betrayal, a flicker of relief warms me.

Ben looks to me; I nod. "We want that list now. Nobody leaves this room until you hand over every name you invited."

Jude nods quickly, then nearly bumps me as he rushes to his computer. Watching him type, it feels like he's desperate to clear his name—fast.

But even if he proves he had no hand in Jasper's death, it doesn't erase the fact he's running an illegal gambling ring aboard our ship.

Illegal gambling beats murder charges, though.

The clatter of keys fills the room as Jude pulls up the list.

We wait, tension sharp, hearts pounding, for the names to appear.

The printer whirs to life. Minutes later, the much-needed list—almost twenty names—is handed to me.

The glaring names jump out: Benson, Chase, Joe, Ida, and more. Some we've seen in the actual tournaments, others are new to us.

"Do you know if they still have their gold chips?" I ask, pushing to speed up our hunt for Jasper's killer. Sorting through twenty-something names means days of interviews and dead ends.

Jude reaches for the list again, highlighting several names. "These ones already played in our tournament—they handed back their gold chips."

I don't want to linger on this illegal tournament. Not now. I shove it to the back of my mind and focus on the paper. Over half the names remain; only eight new ones are highlighted.

Those eight are off the suspect list. After all, whoever left the chips on Jasper's eyes would still have to be holding theirs.

I run my finger down the list, counting eleven names—excluding Benson, since we already have his chip—who still have theirs. Once again, our suspects circle back.

I turn to the group. "Cole, Julia, I need you to dig up everything you can on this other tournament."

From the corner of my eye, Jude's mouth opens, like he's about to protest—but he stops.

Cole nods. "Consider it done."

Julia offers a weak smile and nods, too.

"We'll start interviewing these... invitees," I say, locking eyes with Ben.

Without wasting a second, Ben, Rex, and I coordinate with security to track down the new names. Some we find in their rooms, others in the dining hall, coffee shops, and restaurants.

For the next two hours, we grill them about the gold chip invite. Unaware it's illegal, every single one casually shows us their chips and answers our questions.

Now, just three names remain on the list—Chase, Joe, and Ida. Our main suspects.

I have a sinking feeling one—or all three—of them conspired to kill Jasper.

It's just a matter of finding who wrapped that drawstring tight enough around Jasper's neck to end his life.

Chapter 25

Buzz. The doorbell outside Ida's room rings, faint but urgent from the hallway where Ben, Rex, and I stand, surrounded by nervous energy.

That revelation with Jude still stings, a bitter taste rolling in my mouth, nausea creeping up like I'm about to lose it. Or maybe it's just the ship—this floor beneath my feet—bobbing harder than usual, tossing us like we're on a raft.

Stronger than usual. Like tiny riptides tugging this giant ship under.

That's exactly how my stomach feels—pulled, twisting, struggling to keep me afloat.

Ben and I exchange a quick glance, then the door to Ida's double deluxe suite swings open.

Ida stands there, hair a tangled mess in a loose bun, dried mascara streaked beneath tired eyes, wearing what looks like the same dress from last night. She scans us with a mix of dismay and exhaustion. "Oh, it's just you guys... again. What do you want now?"

I peek past her shoulder at the chaos behind her: clothes strewn across the bed and furniture, shoes scattered like forgotten footprints, bottles of toners, moisturizers, sunscreens—every surface a cluttered mess.

"How are you feeling today, Miss Birch?" Ben asks politely, though we've all had enough small talk this morning.

Ida's skeptical. "Is this some kind of welfare check...?" She scoffs. "Why is the captain of the ship—of all people—checking on me this morning?"

"Well, wouldn't you rather a quick chat before the serious questions come?" I force a smile, but it's hollow.

She looks worn out, like last night drained her dry. "Can we do this later? After I've showered or something?"

Ben doesn't budge. "We'll keep it short. Can we come in?"

She surveys the mess, hesitates. "Uh... maybe not."

Before she can suggest otherwise, Rex slips inside, tugging at my leash.

"Hey!" Ida exclaims as Rex ducks between the door and her leg.

Using that distraction, I push the door wider and step inside. "Sorry about my dog, Miss Birch."

She sighs and steps aside. "Well, come on in, I guess... not that I'm excusing the mess, since you're intruding."

Rex starts sniffing around, probably hunting for crumbs beneath the chaos.

"Where's your roommate?" I ask, glancing around. Even the balcony—overlooking the white ripples trailing the hull—is empty.

"Alice?" Ida shrugs, half-interested. "She said she's getting frozen yogurt or something. But I'm sure you're not here for yogurt... or Alice. So, what is it?"

I pull the gold chip from my pocket and hold it between my fingers. "Is this familiar to you, Miss Birch?"

Her eyes flicker over it, expression unreadable. "You mean a poker chip? Trick question?"

She lets out a hollow chuckle, like it's a game she's done playing.

"If we're being literal, yes, it's a poker chip," I say flatly. "But this one isn't just any chip. I believe you got this in the mail before the cruise. You were invited to another poker tournament, right?"

Her eyes blink—once, twice—like her brain's catching up. Then a flicker of recognition. "Oh, that..."

"So you remember?"

"I did get something like that." She snorts, half-hearted. "But obviously, it wasn't important enough to stick in my memory."

"But you know what it is, don't you?" My suspicion grows. Compared to the other passengers who knew nothing about the chip's shady side, Ida seems cagey.

Does she know about the illegal poker operation?

Or did she lose her gold chip... maybe over Jasper's body?

I hold those questions back for now.

Her body shifts, discomfort creeping in as she rubs her bare arms like a cold draft slipped in. "Like you said, it's an invitation. Tacky, if you ask me."

Ben picks up on her unease. "Can we see the invite?"

Ida's shoulders tense, curling inward like she's trying to make herself smaller. She breaks eye contact, scanning the clutter. "I'd show you if I could find it under all this... mess."

"Want me to call housekeeping?" I offer, aiming to break through the lie.

"Uh, and let her see my underwear and whatever else? No thanks." She crosses her arms over her chest protectively. "I can clean it up myself."

Ben and I both know she's lying. She's hiding something.

"And then you'll find the invite?" I tilt my head, suspicion sharpened.

"If I can find it," she breathes.

"It's not here, is it?" I drop the friendly act.

She stares a moment, then frowns. "Like I said, it's not important. I don't care where it is—here, there, home, the ocean…"

"You know something, don't you?" The words escape before I stop myself.

The ship shudders—a rogue wave rocking us. Items shift, and Ida almost stumbles.

She clears her throat, regaining a bit of composure. "Know what? That I lost the invite? Why does that matter?"

"It matters because—"

Bark! Bark!

Rex's sudden yip cuts me off mid-sentence. The sound comes from the bathroom.

I don't even see him slip away, but his urgency makes me turn toward the open bathroom door.

Ida steps in front of me. "What are you doing?"

I narrow my eyes. "Getting my dog. That's all."

"I'll get him," she offers, but as she moves toward the bathroom, Ben steps forward, gently pushing her aside, letting himself in.

Ida stumbles back, surprised. I slip in right behind Ben.

The cluttered bathroom might overwhelm at first glance, but my attention zeroes in on Rex, standing at the bathtub, hidden behind the closed shower curtain.

"This is highly inappropriate!" Ida's voice snaps behind us, sharp and annoyed.

I don't let her rattle me. I stride straight to the bathtub and pull the shower curtain aside.

There it is—a bag. The same black bag I saw once before... with Jasper.

The night he left the casino.

The night he was murdered.

The same bag he lost to those five hooded men.

The one we've been hunting for ever since.

And now it's just sitting here—in Ida's bathtub.

Half-zipped, neither bursting at the seams nor stuffed like when Jasper carried it out from the cashier's cage.

I still remember how heavy that bag looked, filled to the brim as Jasper casually carried it out.

Now, it sits here—hundreds, maybe thousands—of dollars already spent.

My knees threaten to buckle, but Ida's scream yanks me back. "What the hell do you think you're doing?!"

She storms toward me, but Ben steps in, extending his arm to hold her back.

I take a steady breath and spin to face her. Her eyes are wide—wider than before—and rawer than the guarded ones she showed us earlier.

I step forward, firm. "You're coming with us to the conference room. We have questions."

She recoils, voice sharp. "Come with you? No way!"

I pull the handcuffs from my jeans pocket and dangle them. "Or... I can cuff you and let you walk out in that dress from last night. We can do this easy—or humiliating, Miss Birch."

Her breath hitches. Her eyes drift back to the bathtub. "Can I at least put on a decent coat?"

"That's the last favor you're getting," I say flatly, keeping my anger—mostly pent-up frustration—in check.

Did I really believe her confession of love for Jasper as proof of innocence?

Now, I'm doubting myself.

With that, Ben and I let her slip on the coat and escort her out. Straight to the conference room, where the interrogation begins.

We sit her down and switch on the recorder. I sit across, biting my lower lip until it tastes faintly of iron—a small self-punishment for not seeing this sooner.

I speak. "That money bag... it's Jasper's, isn't it?"

Ida doesn't meet my eyes. Instead, she stares at the table like dust motes swirl in the air.

"Miss Birch, we know it's his," I press, trying to catch her gaze. She won't look. "How did you get it?"

Did she murder him with four others?

That's the answer I want.

But she says nothing.

The ship vibrates beneath me, the morning wearing me down. Midday looks no better.

Despite finding Jasper's bag, I feel defeated by how long it took.

Still, I push. The words murder and kill have to come from her.

"Did you take the bag from Jasper himself?" I nudge. "Did someone bring it to you? We need to know, Miss Birch."

Ida pulls a loose thread on her coat, eyes glued to the table, silent.

For a moment, I let the silence wash over me. Maybe I need it to gather myself.

I feel fury and dismay swirl inside. My fists clench and unclench.

Ben senses it and touches my shoulder softly. "How about you step out? I'll try talking to Ida."

"No, I'm fine," I lie, palms prickling.

Ben shakes his head. I don't look fine. But I keep my face steady.

"I need to do something or else…"

"Find Alice, how about that?" Ben suggests. "Maybe she can help get Ida to talk."

Of course—a trusted confidant.

I know I need to step away before the walls close in. I push my chair back and stand.

Clipping Rex's leash, I say, "I'll be back with Alice."

Ben nods, worried but trusting. I appreciate him letting me step out.

But I don't stroll the ship. My eyes scan for Alice.

I radio security to speed the search.

Instead of a location, Julia replies, "Miss Dela Cruz? Head back to the casino. We found something… and I don't think you'll like it."

Chapter 26

Rex and I blur past the hallways and lounges; the constant hum of the ship fades away in my ringing ears. The clicking of cabin doors, murmurs of nearby conversations, even bursts of laughter from friends and families—all of it mutes into a dull backdrop.

After Julia's message crackled over the radio, I have only one goal—to reach the casino as fast as I can.

But when I get there, the whirring, clicking, snapping, and clattering sounds feel secondary.

The noise can't cut through the fog of worry clouding my mind. My senses shrink to a tight bubble of focus, blocking everything else out.

I head straight to the back of the room and turn toward the manager's office. Jude stands in the corner, nervous and biting his nails. Cole and Julia huddle over spreadsheets filled with rows and columns of numbers.

Financial records—I can tell at a glance. Still, I ask, "What are we looking at?"

Julia glances at Jude, who shoots upright. "I can explain, Miss Dela—"

"How about you let the women talk?" Cole interrupts sharply, glaring at Jude like he's shrinking under the weight of suspicion.

Julia grabs my elbow and pulls me close, pointing to the printouts. "We've been going through these for two hours. There are a lot of... discrepancies."

"Clerical errors, that's all," Jude insists, earning another icy look from Cole.

"It's not," Julia whispers. "We're not talking about misplaced decimals or flipped numbers. The casino's only been open a few days, but there are invoices for equipment repairs, and even catering."

Her finger hovers over a line on the second page. "And this? A five-figure bill for carpet cleaning? All the carpets are brand new, and we have in-house staff for that."

Cole slides his documents toward me. "$25,000 was wired to this account a few days ago. I looked it up—it's not a legitimate company. My guess? An offshore account."

Where could Jude have gotten $25,000? That's my biggest question. Surely, he wouldn't just dip into the casino's funds—that'd be too obvious.

Could it be from Jasper's winnings...?

"Okay, okay." Jude steps away from the wall, like he's done hiding. "You're jumping to conclusions. I can explain if you just give me a chance."

"Explain embezzlement?" I snap, the weight of the day pressing down like a boulder on my chest.

"It's not that... it's something else. We just—"

"You just what?" I stand straighter, meeting his eyes. "The casino hasn't even been open a week, and this much discrepancy means this was planned. Calculated. You came here with this purpose, didn't you?"

"I..." Jude trails off, no clever excuse left.

"Was Jasper's death part of the fraud?" I blurt out.

His face drains of color. This time, he doesn't deny it—but doesn't confirm it either. Instead, he presses his lips into a thin line.

"What? No response?" I push.

Jude backs into his corner, eyes glued to the floor. That's a yes.

My throat tightens as everything unravels faster than I can keep up. Layers of trouble inside The Midnight Tide keep peeling back.

The discoveries are promising for Jasper's case—but terrifying for the cruise.

How did all this go unnoticed?

First murder. Now embezzlement?

What's next? A rogue iceberg?

God, I hope not.

"What now?" Cole looks up from the papers.

I turn away from Jude and say, "Take him to the holding cell. I'll ask Ben to meet me there."

Cole nods without hesitation and grabs Jude's arm, leading him out. Jude glances back once, mouth closed tight.

As they leave, I tell Julia, "Go to the conference room and stay with Ida. Ben's there. I need him to make decisions about... all this."

I gesture weakly at the printouts.

Julia offers a faint smile and heads out, leaving Rex and me staring down the mess Jude left behind.

The numbers mock me—the fake expenses, the phantom bills. How far does Jude's operation go? From gold chips on his desk to these records—could it all connect to Jasper's murder?

I gather the papers, slide them into an empty envelope I find on Jude's desk, and head to the ship's only holding area—a grim place where the drone of machinery drowns out everything, and the exhaust fumes cling to the skin.

It smells of rust and dampness, a stench no disinfectant can mask.

This is the hidden underbelly of the ship—a place passengers never see. No luxury here. Just bare walls, sticky floors, and flickering yellow lights.

Rex and I arrive to find Ben and Cole whispering outside the holding cell. Between the ship's vibration and the ocean slapping the hull, they could shout and still be unheard.

I approach them, envelope tucked under my arm. "Heard about Jude?"

Ben perks up, turning toward me, weariness etched on his face. A captain steering a ship through stormy waters—except the sharks are inside.

"Cole gave me a briefing," Ben says. "Are those the documents?"

I hand him the envelope. He peeks inside, already weighed down by the thick stack.

After flipping through the edges, Ben asks, "Think this ties to Jasper?"

"I wish I knew," I say, nodding toward the holding cell door. "Maybe Jude can shed some light."

Ben nods slowly.

Cole adds, "I had my men retrieve Jasper's money bag. I'm heading to the office to see if it's short by $25,000. Then we'll know for sure."

"Thanks, Cole." It's all I can say.

While Cole exits the lower decks, Ben, Rex, and I step into the holding area.

The room looks just as cramped as I remember—an old couch and a battered coffee table sit outside the holding cell, which contains a makeshift bed, a stainless-steel sink, and a toilet, all squeezed into the tight space behind metal bars.

Jude already looks uncomfortable. As soon as he sees us, he clings to the bars and snaps, "This is inhumane, don't you think? Locking up a casino manager like a... wild animal!"

Rex growls low.

I meet Jude's gaze. "You know what sets us apart from wild animals? Morality—the ability to tell right from wrong."

Ben adds, "Everyone here knows illegal gambling is wrong, Jude. This holding cell is... fitting."

The crease between Jude's brows deepens. "Oh, don't be ridiculous! This is illegal detainment at best!"

Ben slaps the thick envelope of financial records onto the scratched coffee table. "You know illegal better than we do. So, why don't you tell us what we need to know, and we'll let you out. Then the police can figure out what comes next."

Jude scoffs, backing away and plopping onto the not-so-soft mattress. "Right, because that's so much better for me."

I lean in. "Did you think we wouldn't hand you over after the evidence we found?"

He seals his lips shut like he's mocking me—just like in his office.

I sigh, holding back frustration. "Not talking again?"

Ben steps forward. "Jude, you'll get more out of cooperating. We don't know how far this goes, but right now, it looks bad for you. Help us, and we can tell the police you cooperated. That's a mitigating circumstance—it helps your case."

Jude just huffs and looks away.

Ben glances at me. I shrug. "He didn't want to talk to me earlier, either. What do you want to do, Captain?"

Ben thinks it over, silent long enough for Jude to glance at him nervously. Then Ben says, "If he won't talk, we shut down the casino and search it top to bottom. Suspend operations if we have to. Leave no stone unturned."

His certainty surprises me—it's a fast decision for something so huge.

Jude's eyes widen like marbles, jaw tight. He's clearly decided to stay silent.

"Guard outside this room," I tell Jude. "If you change your mind, ask him to call us. Until then, we'll check in again tonight."

With that, Ben, Rex, and I leave the holding area feeling in control. Jude's expression is satisfying, but the work's not done.

Within the hour, Ben shuts down casino operations. Cole and his team arrive, methodical and grim.

Gone is the lively hum of slot machines, chatter, and cards—only ventilation's soft drone and our footsteps fill the space.

Besides the fake supplier and offshore account we found, Cole's team digs for solid evidence. They empty Jude's office drawers, shift furniture, and lift carpets. They knock on walls to check for hidden compartments. Others pore over Jude's digital devices.

Rex pulls me toward the cashier's vault, where a few others already inspect the room. The compact space smells like fresh money. Steel walls and doors surround us.

Locked compartments and metal shelves line the walls. A small table holds labeled chip trays and a money-counting machine. But Rex's focus is elsewhere.

He paws insistently at the lower right compartment, whining convincingly.

I get the attention of the staff waiting nearby. Seconds later, the employee unlocks it—and inside are stacks of high-denomination chips.

I blink at them, wondering why this batch's been separated.

Before long, another officer approaches, wielding a UV light. The chips glow—counterfeit.

A low whisper behind me. Cole strides in, half-disgusted, half-impressed. "This is a well-planned operation, Rose."

"What else?" I ask, suddenly dry-mouthed.

Cole pauses, building suspense. "Multiple surveillance clips show suspicious activity—players winning at unusually high rates on the same tables with the same dealers."

I scoff, disbelief bubbling.

In just days, Jude's not just skimming—he's running a full illegal gambling scheme, far beyond clerical errors.

Leaving Cole to work, I rejoin Ben at Jude's office, where laptops, tablets, and phones are under scrutiny.

Ben's stern face tells me another shock awaits.

"What is it?" I ask.

Ben pulls a laptop closer. On the screen is a messaging app I don't recognize. Jude's username: "Mr. Manager." The other user: "ecaeht."

I read the latest message: Make sure no one finds out. Just follow everything I taught you so far.

My breath catches. This has to be the bigger player—Jude's puppeteer, pulling all the strings.

Chapter 27

The day burns out like a candle wick to a flame. But even as the evening lulls most to sleep, I'm nowhere near calling it a night—or even calling it a day. Crazy hardly covers it.

Too many things are spinning out all at once.

Julia tells me Ida's still refusing to talk. In the holding area, Jude's desperate to get his hands on a phone, begging to call someone. Unaware he's already past salvation—we've uncovered too much for anyone to save him, even if he cooperates.

While Ben checks on Jude, I head to one of the ship's cafés, where Alice is waiting.

Salt air tangles in my hair as I join her in the café's open seating. Her steaming coffee looks cold in the constant wind. More than that, Alice shivers in her chair, clutching herself like a thin coat won't cut the chill.

She avoids the starry sky spilling over the dark ocean—the beauty too much to bear right now.

I sit across from her. Alice finally asks, "Is Ida alright?"

"She is," I say. "But I don't know how much longer she'll keep silent. Do you know why we brought her in?"

Alice shakes her head, voice low. "I asked around, but everyone tells me to ask you. Still, I have my guesses."

"Which are?" I lean forward, wind biting the side of my face but I don't care.

"For starters, the stolen money…" Alice breaks eye contact, embarrassed. "I checked our room. The money bag's gone."

"So you knew?" Disappointment slides through me. I thought Alice was more reliable than Ida—considering how she cared after Ida's blackout. But here we are.

Alice nods slowly, sighing. "Look, I don't want trouble. I only came because Ida promised me—'all expenses paid,' she said. If I'd known about the shady stuff, I wouldn't have come. But I was already here. Some might say I'm an accomplice."

"Accomplice to what?" My heart skips.

Is this where Alice confesses Ida's role in Jasper's murder?

She breathes out, "The theft, I guess…"

My heart sinks. "The theft? The money bag?"

Not the murder? a tiny voice nags.

Alice hesitates, hands wrapped around the cold mug.

"If you weren't involved," I offer, "you won't get in more trouble."

"Even if I knew and stayed quiet?"

"Even then."

Alice searches my eyes for lies but finds none. She sighs, then spills, "Ida… and a few casino people… planned to steal Jasper's winnings."

I hold my breath, the fog lifting. "Who?"

Alice's face crumples, torn between loyalty and guilt. She chooses guilt. "I don't know them all. But there's Benson Wolf, the casino manager, and four others."

There it is.

The confirmation that we're on the right path.

I don't let relief show—not yet. "And the plan… was to steal Jasper's money? No matter what?"

Alice squints. "What do you mean?"

"Did they mean to get the money by any means? Even... killing Jasper?" I tread carefully.

Alice's face drains of color, pale as ash.

She stammers, "Jasper was killed?"

"You didn't know?" Shock, confusion, regret, and anger flash across her face.

"No, not at all!" she says, voice high. "I... I don't think Ida knew either. Maybe the plan was just to steal Jasper's winnings because he cheats. Then split the money. Ida joined out of spite—she hates Jasper for dumping her. She wanted to get his attention, not... not this."

The rawness in her voice shows innocence. But also guilt—for staying silent, for letting her friend dive into darkness.

Alice looks like she might cry, fighting it back. I offer to walk her back to their suite.

Then I head to the conference room to face Ida—armed now with a way to break through.

I tell Julia to call it a night and find Ida sitting there, her food untouched. She looks worse for wear—dry, smudged lipstick; hair wild despite the low bun.

All day, she's held firm—arms crossed, legs folded tight, lips sealed and chapped.

I've had enough. I dive in. "Did you know Jasper's dead?"

I almost flinch at the harshness, but it's either this or more hours of silence.

Ida snaps her eyes up, breaking her vow. "What?"

"So you didn't know," I say, leaning back. "That night, when you and your friends planned to steal Jasper's winnings—you didn't just take his money. You took his life."

Her eyes widen further, tears pooling fast. They fall like waterfalls down her cheeks. She swats at them with shaking hands but can't stop the flood.

The walls Ida built all day crumble in seconds.

The act is over.

I slide a box of tissues toward her but she ignores it, wiping with the backs of her hands.

"I'm sorry you had to hear it this way," I say softly. "But I've already talked to Alice. She told me everything she knows. Now, it's your turn."

I give Ida a moment to gather herself. She takes a tissue, dabs at her eyes, sobbing into it before dropping it onto the soggy roll in front of her. Then she whispers, "That wasn't the plan. Jasper wasn't supposed to..."

Her voice cracks, tears spilling again.

After a beat, I say, "He wasn't supposed to die. Yet he did, Ida. That night—the person who broke into Jasper's room? He killed Jasper and took the money. Didn't anyone tell you that part?"

"No! No one told me..." Ida's hands clutch the tissue tightly. "I... I don't understand. That's not what we agreed on!"

"What did you agree on?" I press.

Now the truth has broken through, Ida can't stop herself. "We were only supposed to take the money and split it."

"Who's 'we'?"

"Me, Jude, Benson, Chase, Joe, Rocco, and Fuller," she lists, voice heavy with grief, her brain fogged by tears.

Lucky for us, all suspects fall on one list, now with two new names—Rocco and Fuller.

The five hooded men—and two more accomplices. But who's who? Who pulled the drawstring around Jasper's neck?

I keep going. "And Rocco and Fuller—who are they?"

"They're casino dealers," Ida admits, fresh tears falling. "They work closely with Jude."

"Were they two of the five men who went to Jasper's suite?"

I feel guilty twisting the knife of Ida's heartbreak, but it has to be done.

She nods. "Yeah, they were off duty that night. Their job was to wait for Benson, Chase, and Joe, then hand over hoodies so they could head to Jasper's suite as planned."

Even with the names in hand, I don't feel relief. Knowing seven people colluded to commit a crime churns my stomach.

How can there be this much evil on one ship?

It makes me want to vomit.

I swallow past the nausea and focus back on Ida. "Which one went into Jasper's room?"

"I... I don't know! It was one of them!" she snaps. "Can I at least know where Jasper is?"

"His body was taken to the last port of call," I say.

"Did he... did he suffer?" Ida breaks down, but keeps her eyes on me, desperate for the answer.

But how do you answer that?

Who doesn't suffer at the hands of their murderer?

I can only say, "I don't know, Ida. But your confession is helping us find Jasper's killer."

"I can't believe this!" Ida cries, burying her face in her hands. "This wasn't supposed to happen."

I stand, hesitating before resting a reluctant hand on her back, gently rubbing her shoulders. "I'm so sorry, Ida."

She scoffs, hollow. "Well, an apology won't bring Jasper back, will it?"

"You're right," I sigh, heavy. "But we can at least bring justice for his death."

And for the first time in days, I believe it.

We're no longer chasing shadows. This time, we're hunting real men—men with real reasons to kill.

Chapter 28

The tension in the room is thick—you can almost see the heat swirling in the air as the larger conference room slowly fills. Benson Wolf, Chase Ford, Joe Booker, Rocco West, and Fuller Lee enter one by one, each brought in separately, but none acknowledging the others, as if insisting they don't know each other.

From the security cameras, Cole, Ben, and I watch the five men settle into their seats, forced into proximity but connected only by what's unspoken. Benson swings one leg over the other, bored. Chase and Joe exchange glances, shrug, or flash unreadable expressions. Rocco—tall, dark-skinned, with sharp gray eyes—scans the room, his gaze lingering on the blue backdrop beyond the windows: the ocean and the approaching outline of Basseterre.

Even the city's sandy shores and green foothills offer me no comfort.

My eyes flick to Fuller Lee, the other casino dealer, who fidgets with a button on his shirt.

Beneath the table, a recorder waits to catch every word. But for now, all we hear are scraping chairs, sniffles, and someone clearing his throat. Ben and I decide it's time to intervene.

As we step inside, the atmosphere shifts—thick with sweat, perfume, and aftershave. The air feels heavier here, warmer than the hallways outside. Though the room boasts a stunning ocean view, even that fades behind the weight of this tense gathering.

"Thank you for taking the time to join us," I say, sitting down beside Ben across the table from them.

Benson smirks, "We didn't really have much of a choice."

Chase's tone is sharp. "Why are we here again? And what's with all these... other people?"

I nod at Chase, pulling out a notebook. "No need for introductions. Let's get to why we're here. Anyone want to guess?"

Fuller answers, "Is it about the casino operations being suspended?"

Chase scoffs without meeting Fuller's eyes. "Yeah, I wondered about that too..."

Ben leans forward, voice low and steady. "That... and more. To be frank, we have a killer among us. And we think he's sitting right here."

I watch their faces carefully. Benson remains unreadable—clearly already in the know. Chase's jaw tightens. Joe blinks in surprise. Rocco's brow furrows. Fuller tilts his head, curious.

Unlike Ida, none of them react strongly. Maybe the name will hit harder.

"Jasper Thorne died shortly after winning the tournament on night one," I say.

Silence. Frowns deepen. No gasps, no sudden movements.

Benson shrugs. "I thought we cleared it up that it wasn't me. Can I leave now?"

Joe leans forward, eyes narrowing at Benson. "Wait—you knew?"

"I was told not long ago," Benson admits coolly.

"And you didn't tell me?" Joe's shock surfaces. It doesn't make him innocent—none of these five are.

Ben interrupts, "We asked Mr. Wolf to keep quiet."

Joe hesitates, biting back something. "Yeah, but…"

"But what, Mr. Booker?" I prompt, watching for any slip.

He exhales, sinking back. "Doesn't matter."

Only the ship's engines and ocean waves fill the pause—until Rocco breaks the silence.

"So, a passenger dies onboard, and you bring us here because you think one of us did it…?"

"That's our working theory," Ben says, voice clipped but professional. "And it's based on solid information, not just rumor. The casino manager is currently in custody—suspected of involvement in Jasper's murder and illegal gambling. We believe you all know something about that."

Ben's gaze sharpens on Rocco and Fuller—the shady dealers tied to Jude, apart from this group.

Rocco looks away quickly. Fuller shifts in his chair.

The room tightens with discomfort.

"Anyone want to confess to Jasper's murder?" I ask.

If only it were that easy.

Of course, no one answers.

Ben and I exchange a glance. We've wasted enough time trying to coax talk out of them.

We stand.

"We'll return when you're ready to confess," I say.

No words follow as we exit. Now it's just a waiting game—someone will crack or slip up. Unknown to them, we're watching from the security office.

Ben heads to the bridge to oversee disembarkation.

I contact Julia. Ida's been a crying mess all morning, holed up in her room. Jude keeps asking for a lawyer—he can wait.

Right now, my focus narrows: who among these five will break first?

Outside Cole's office on the promenade deck, Basseterre's metropolis spreads out—deep green hills, towering trees, and bright bougainvillea greeting the ship's arrival.

Beyond the sandy coast, colonial buildings peek through foliage, almost welcoming.

But no colorful awnings or tropical scents distract me from the monitor in front of me.

Thirty minutes pass. Passengers disembark. The five men stay tight-lipped, only moving to grab water or help themselves to the cookie box we left.

Chase mutters something about not enjoying his vacation, then slumps back.

Benson tries to leave, but a guard blocks him.

An hour ticks by.

Still nothing.

Eventually, Stacy shows up to check on us. With no risk of her identity being revealed to those men in the conference room, she's free to move about—but she chooses to stay close, lingering with Cole and me.

Another twenty minutes drag by.

Just when I start thinking nothing will happen this morning, Chase finally snaps. "Alright! Who the hell here killed Jasper?"

"Shut up, Chase," Joe cuts in quickly, nudging him and jerking his chin toward the guard stationed outside. They should be more worried about the hidden camera and the recorder under the table than the guard.

"Well, I want out of here." Chase lowers his voice, but Cole just cranks up the volume on his computer. Chase continues, "I didn't even know Jasper was dead. That's not what we agreed on."

"It's not," Benson replies coolly, feet propped on the table. "But keep talking like that, and they'll find out we all conspired to steal his money. That might sound better than murder, but it's still a crime."

"Yeah, but we can just return the money—no big deal," Chase argues. "Maybe pay a fine or something. We all have good lawyers, don't we?"

Rocco shrugs, "Some rules don't apply to us, no, sir."

Unlike Benson, Chase, and Joe, Rocco and Fuller are just card dealers, making more money than most thanks to their shady dealings.

"Then I'll find you both a lawyer!" Chase says arrogantly. "Can we just agree on who killed Jasper? I'm pretty sure it's none of us, right? He couldn't have died while we were retrieving the money."

Chase studies Joe closely.

Joe suddenly jumps up and starts pacing.

Cole, Stacy, and I watch the men, waiting for the next shoe to drop.

Fuller spins his chair toward Joe. "You went into that room, right? Did you...?"

He trails off.

I feel my back straighten, ready to bolt.

Joe falls silent. Then, after a beat, he says, "Let's just say I killed Jasper, okay? Can we drop it?"

As we step inside, the atmosphere shifts—thick with sweat, perfume, and aftershave. The air feels heavier here, warmer than the hallways outside. Though the room boasts a stunning ocean view, even that fades behind the weight of this tense gathering.

"Thank you for taking the time to join us," I say, sitting down beside Ben across the table from them.

Benson smirks, "We didn't really have much of a choice."

Chase's tone is sharp. "Why are we here again? And what's with all these... other people?"

I nod at Chase, pulling out a notebook. "No need for introductions. Let's get to why we're here. Anyone want to guess?"

Fuller answers, "Is it about the casino operations being suspended?"

Chase scoffs without meeting Fuller's eyes. "Yeah, I wondered about that too..."

Ben leans forward, voice low and steady. "That... and more. To be frank, we have a killer among us. And we think he's sitting right here."

I watch their faces carefully. Benson remains unreadable—clearly already in the know. Chase's jaw tightens. Joe blinks in surprise. Rocco's brow furrows. Fuller tilts his head, curious.

Unlike Ida, none of them react strongly. Maybe the name will hit harder.

"Jasper Thorne died shortly after winning the tournament on night one," I say.

Silence. Frowns deepen. No gasps, no sudden movements.

Benson shrugs. "I thought we cleared it up that it wasn't me. Can I leave now?"

Joe leans forward, eyes narrowing at Benson. "Wait—you knew?"

"I was told not long ago," Benson admits coolly.

"And you didn't tell me?" Joe's shock surfaces. It doesn't make him innocent—none of these five are.

Ben interrupts, "We asked Mr. Wolf to keep quiet."

Joe hesitates, biting back something. "Yeah, but..."

"But what, Mr. Booker?" I prompt, watching for any slip.

He exhales, sinking back. "Doesn't matter."

Only the ship's engines and ocean waves fill the pause—until Rocco breaks the silence.

"So, a passenger dies onboard, and you bring us here because you think one of us did it...?"

"That's our working theory," Ben says, voice clipped but professional. "And it's based on solid information, not just rumor. The casino manager is currently in custody—suspected of involvement in Jasper's murder and illegal gambling. We believe you all know something about that."

Ben's gaze sharpens on Rocco and Fuller—the shady dealers tied to Jude, apart from this group.

Rocco looks away quickly. Fuller shifts in his chair.

The room tightens with discomfort.

"Anyone want to confess to Jasper's murder?" I ask.

If only it were that easy.

Of course, no one answers.

Ben and I exchange a glance. We've wasted enough time trying to coax talk out of them.

We stand.

"We'll return when you're ready to confess," I say.

It's not an outright confession, but Cole and I don't hesitate. We rush out of the room.

If Joe entered Jasper's room, it makes sense he's the killer. Those few minutes after he left is when I found Jasper's body.

Cole and I storm back into the conference room. I nearly stumble as we hurry. Cole grabs Joe by the elbows and leads him out.

Before we even get far, I step in front of Joe and demand, "Did you really kill Jasper?"

"What... how... were you listening?!" Joe snaps, wiggling slightly from Cole's grip.

"Well? Did you kill him?" I raise my voice, trying to intimidate him.

Joe awkwardly adjusts his glasses, scanning the room. "I... I said that because I'm the one who entered Jasper's room!"

"And that's exactly when you killed him!" I argue, confused by his hesitation.

"No, I'm..." He pauses, exhales, then lowers his voice to a whisper. "I'm scared of what might happen if I tell the truth."

I take a step back but push forward. "More scared of going to jail for murdering Jasper Thorne?"

Frustrated, Joe rubs his eyes, pressing his palm to them. "Can you promise I'll be safe if I tell you?"

Without hesitation, I nod. We'll do everything to protect our passengers. "You can trust us."

He releases Cole's arm. "Fine. When I got into Jasper's room, someone else was already there. Same hoodie. He'd knocked Jasper unconscious. Said Jude worked for him, and if I said a word, he'd come after me next."

Joe glances nervously down the empty hallway, paranoia thick in his voice.

My brain kicks into overdrive. Jude's boss has to be the one he messaged about illegal gambling.

That means he's here. On the ship.

And all we have is a username—ecaeht.

"Who is he?" I ask carefully, feeling Joe's anxiety rub off on me.

Joe sighs shallowly. "I don't know his real name. Jude says he only uses a codename."

"A codename?" I repeat, a chill running down my spine.

I've heard that before.

Joe continues, "Jude says he works for The Ace—the mastermind behind all this. I'm pretty sure he killed Jasper too."

My skin prickles with goosebumps. Suddenly, the username makes sense—The Ace, spelled backward.

We never checked if someone else left Jasper's room before or after the incident. Maybe The Ace was waiting inside, slipping out just before I arrived.

If Joe's right, Jasper's killer has been circling us all along, fooling us into trust.

Wide-eyed, I turn to Cole. "Max Parrish—did he leave the ship?"

Chapter 29

"He's not here," Julia confirms as we rush out of the ship—Ben, Cole, Stacy, Julia, Rex, and me.

It's been two hours since The Midnight Tide docked at Basseterre.

Two long hours since Max disappeared—and he could've slipped away for good, leaving us with a mess of crimes to clean up on our own.

The thought makes me run faster down the gangway. "We have to find him," I tell the group.

Cole shakes his head. "You all go ahead. I'll coordinate with the police. Make sure Max doesn't leave the island—one way or another."

While Stacy stays with Cole, I nod and keep moving, eyes scanning every face for even a hint of Max.

"I'll check the beach," Julia offers, her yellow visor hat perched perfectly. Honestly, I'm too wound up to compliment her on the matching romper. So Ben and I head toward the shops.

Rex leads without hesitation, tugging at his leash like a bloodhound on the scent.

"You think he's tracking Max's trail?" Ben asks.

I barely have the breath to think, but I nod. "I think so."

I trust Rex's instincts, letting him pull me wherever he wants—hoping it leads to Max.

When Rex suddenly stops in front of an ice cream cake shop, I deflate a little.

Maybe all those sweet treats just caught his attention.

Still, I scan the alfresco tables—no sign of Max. "I don't think he's here, bud. Want a cold treat—"

"There!" Ben points inside, where Max lounges like a kid rewarded after a dentist visit, spoon halfway to his mouth, grinning like it's all fun and games.

I push through the chilly shop, eyes locked on Max. The pastel décor and white furniture blur around him. He catches us coming in, thanks to the chime overhead, and beams.

"Rose! Captain!" Max waves, like nothing's wrong.

But I'm not fooled.

I hand Rex's leash to Ben and step closer. "Get up."

"Oh, you've got to try this marshmallow chocolate fudge—"

"I said, get up." I grab Max's arm and pull the handcuffs from my back pocket.

His face drains as the metal catches the light. "Whoa, whoa. What's this, Rose?"

"No more games. You're under arrest for the murder of—"

Before I finish, Max doubles over, knocking his chair over. Curious customers turn to us. Regaining balance, he backs into the wall. "What are you talking about? You know I didn't do it!"

I study him—fear flooding his face, pupils dilated, sweat shining even in the cold air, hands trembling but clenched tight.

"If you're innocent," I say, voice low, "why does my witness swear they saw you inside Jasper's room that night? When Jasper was just there for the money bag? You taunted him, admitted Jude's working for you with that nasty little gambling ring, and threatened to kill him if he ever said he saw you."

I don't care if innocent ears hear. I want this over. I want The Midnight Tide free of poison. To cleanse the ship, as they say.

I want our glory back.

We've let one immoral man poison our casino long enough. I want a do-over.

I'm itching to cuff Max and end this nightmare.

Still, he edges closer to the wall like it might swallow him. "That's not me, Rose! Come on!"

"You're suddenly not The Ace?" I taunt, stepping in as he scrambles upright.

"Well, I'm The Ace! Just not the one in Jasper's room that night, I swear!" His words jumble, and it grates on my nerves.

I reach for his wrist again. He raises his hands. "Fine! I'm not The Ace! I'm a... fraud!"

The confession drops like a bomb, silencing the room. Even the laughter and chatter from outside fade.

My arms go slack at my sides.

Max lowers his guard and explains, voice shaky. "I... I've been using The Ace's name to feel important. Yeah, I'm a card shark, but not like the real deal. Just a copycat. I like how people treat me when I say I'm the legendary Ace... even though I'm not."

Stunned, I flash back to our brief talks—him admitting to his other identity, helping Stacy win that poker tournament like a pro. I ask, "You really expect me to believe that?"

"It's the truth." His voice drops, embarrassed. "You have to believe the truth, right?"

"But how can I…" I trail off, struggling to make sense of it all.

"Because The Ace is my son."

The voice cuts through the silence—a woman I hadn't noticed rises from a chair nearby. Her huge sun hat hides half her face.

Ben looks at her. "Excuse me, but you are…?"

"Melissa Ferris," she says. "I believe we're on the same ship, Captain. I came with my son—the real Ace."

My eyes dart between her and Max, torn about who to trust.

Why else would a random passenger jump into a murder arrest conversation?

So, I end up staring at Melissa, an early-sixties-something woman dressed like she's stepped right out of the 1950s.

Melissa walks over to Ben and says, "Am I right in thinking The Ace murdered another passenger on the ship?"

Gasps ripple from the bystanders nearby—everyone's eavesdropping now, unable to mind their own business.

Ben nods slowly. "You heard right, Mrs. Ferris. We have a credible eyewitness who saw The Ace inside the very room where it happened."

Melissa lets out a dramatic sigh. "Well, I've always known my son's tangled up in plenty of crimes—mostly gambling-related. And sure, I've turned a blind eye when it meant funding my lifestyle. But murder? That's where I draw the line."

I swear I can hear her heart breaking at those words—a mother reaching her limit with the child she's tried to protect.

We all let that sink in for a moment. Then Melissa says, "I know where The Ace is. I'll bring you to him myself."

The Midnight Tide is as quiet as it can be, with most passengers off exploring the island. Waves crash against the shore, seagulls cry overhead, and soft music drifts from the Sunrise Bar—a cozy spot inside the ship overlooking the sea—as we head back onboard.

Melissa leads the way and stops at the bar's doorway, her sandaled feet planted firmly on the carpet. She points to a suited man sipping whiskey on the rocks. "That's my son—Walton Ferris, better known as The Ace."

I glance at Melissa, catching only one of her eyes beneath her wide-brimmed hat. It glistens with unshed tears. "Are you sure about turning your son in, Mrs. Ferris?"

"Well, this breaks my heart," she admits. "But I haven't been the best mother. I've helped him with plenty of illegal things for money—but not murder."

I let out a heavy sigh. Even Rex whimpers softly at her words.

Max trails behind us like a lost puppy. He stays quiet, but I can tell from his downcast eyes he feels that mother's pain in the air.

I turn my attention back to the man at the bar—the well-dressed figure who finally puts a face to The Ace.

And Jasper's killer.

Now that he's here, I feel my nerves tighten. What else is waiting for us when we arrest him?

Ben squeezes my hand, reading my anxiety. "Want me to talk to him?"

I shake my head. This is something I have to handle. "No. I'll do it."

Melissa speaks quietly. "Is it alright if I leave? I just can't watch my son get... arrested. But I'll be in my suite if you need me."

"Of course, Mrs. Ferris," I say with a small smile.

She slips away before her son can spot her standing with our suspicious crew.

Ben takes Rex's leash from me and nods for me to go ahead. Even Max sticks close, like a kid afraid of getting lost.

I lead the way, steadying my breath.

Closing the distance to Walton, I see a man with sharp blue eyes, dark hair, and a strong jawline. He glances up, recognizing me. "You're the cruise director, right? Can I help you?"

His eyes flick to Max—familiar, but not lingering.

I steel myself. "It's over, Mr. Ferris. We know about the illegal gambling ring at the casino and the... murder."

Walton doesn't flinch. He swirls his glass, ice cubes clinking lazily, and takes a slow sip.

"Did you hear me?" I press.

Finally, he sets the glass down but keeps his hand resting on it. "I don't know what you want me to say about those accusations."

"Well, you're not denying them, are you?" I snap.

He shrugs, eyes locked on the glass.

I'm done wasting time. I pull out the handcuffs again. "Mr. Ferris, you're under arrest for the murder of Jasper Thorne."

The moment I grab his wrist, Walton hurls his whiskey glass at my feet. Liquid gold and shattered crystal splash across the floor.

That's his chance to bolt.

"Rex!" I shout.

Max pulls me back, away from the shards. Ben charges after Walton, fueled by blind fury.

Walton doesn't get far—he's still inside the Sunrise Bar when Ben tackles him, rolls him to the floor, and pins him down.

I rush over and snap the cuffs on Walton's wrists. He struggles, but between us, he can't break free.

Just then, Cole's voice echoes through the bar. "Rose!"

I look up and see Cole with police officers running toward us—just in time.

The officers haul Walton to his feet and drag him away by the arms. Finally, the man responsible for so much harm is caught.

Ben, breathing hard from the chase, looks at me. "Are you hurt?"

I shake my head, noting my jeans are soaked where the whiskey spilled. "I'm okay."

Stacy storms in, ignoring Walton being led away. She pulls me into a tight hug. "Are you okay?"

"Why does everyone keep asking me that?" I groan, half-laughing.

Tears in her eyes, Stacy steps back. "So, is it over? Did we get Jasper's killer?"

"And the mastermind behind the illegal gambling," I say, smiling. This time, it's real—warm and relieved. The worst is finally behind us.

Epilogue
Two Weeks Later

The afternoon in San Juan unfolds like a watercolor painting stretched across a warm canvas, softened by the Caribbean breeze. The sun drapes a golden glow over the shore's sand where I finally settle onto a sunbed, my body spread out, soaking it all in.

Next to me, Stacy still chases that perfect Caribbean tan, flipping to catch rays on her back. Ben and Cole toss a ball around with Rex nearby, the dog darting eagerly between them. In the distance, Julia—wearing a retro red polka-dot one-piece straight out of the eighties—carries coconut husks brimming with flavored margaritas.

Before us, the turquoise water shimmers in gradients—from pale blue at the shore to deep sapphire where it stretches out to meet the horizon—catching the sunlight like a scattering of tiny stars on the ocean's surface.

No one could guess that just two weeks ago, this group and I hunted down a murderer aboard The Midnight Tide. To anyone watching, we're just tourists, soaking up a well-earned beach vacation.

"This is the life, Rose," Stacy sighs, shifting her position to balance out her tan. "No more chasing killers—just waves and salt air."

I chuckle, letting the steady rhythm of the surf wash over me. "Yeah, this is definitely the payoff."

Julia's soft footsteps draw near. My assistant and friend balances three coconut husks, each topped with a tiny umbrella. "Okay, I've got classic, peach, and strawberry margaritas. Which ones do you want?"

"Let me try the peach," Stacy says, extending her arm weakly, and I hand it to her.

Julia turns to me, cheeks slightly flushed from the sun. "How about you, Rose?"

"You choose first," I tell her.

She considers a moment. "Strawberry, then." She slides the classic margarita my way, and I accept it with a smile.

I take a bittersweet, refreshing sip and try to remember the last time I truly felt at ease—when everything around me felt calm and steady.

Thinking back, I realize I haven't had nearly as many nightmares since solving Jasper's case. Before, they haunted me every night. In the past two weeks, maybe just two or three. And I haven't touched any sleeping aids.

Is it the Caribbean air working its magic? I'd like to believe so. But maybe it's more about accepting that life—and death—unfold as they will. No one, not me or anyone else, can change the course of fate.

As I slowly make peace with life as it is, I find myself lighter—less burdened by guilt or regret.

"You ladies alright?" Ben's voice pulls me back. Sweat gleams on his forehead as he approaches.

"We're good," I say, raising my margarita in a small toast.

Ben heads back with Cole toward the hut-like kiosk to grab their own drinks.

Just as I savor this perfect moment—the sun-drenched shore, the endless blue ocean—my phone buzzes in my bag.

Out of habit, I fish it out, only to get an immediate scolding from Stacy. "Whatever happened to no phones on vacation?"

"Sorry, just checking who it is..." I glance at the screen. An unknown caller ID flashes. Something about it unsettles me, and not answering feels worse. I slip away from the sunbeds. "Hello?"

For a heartbeat, I half-expect Walton's voice—his threats echoing from the other line, promising he'll come back for me. Instead, a cheerful woman answers, "Hi! Is this Rose Dela Cruz?"

Caught off guard by how lively she sounds, I reply, "Oh, hi... yes, this is she."

"My name's Bea," she says, professional and upbeat. "I'm calling from The Gambling Salon in Laughlin, Nevada. We wanted to know if you'd be interested in working with us as an internal investigator."

I blink toward the horizon, confused by the timing. "Uh, if this is about the illegal gambling we uncovered aboard The Midnight Tide, that's strictly part of my job as cruise director. Not exactly a new challenge for me. So thanks, but I'll have to decline."

"Oh, are you sure?" Bea presses. "We're prepared to offer double your current salary."

I keep my tone polite. "Your company can't offer me the people I already work with—and I love my job here, especially the team. So I'm not going anywhere. But I appreciate the offer."

I hang up, exhaling a breath I didn't realize I was holding.

A hand settles on my bare back—it's Ben, returning from the kiosk. "Who was that?"

"Bea from The Gambling Salon in Nevada," I shrug. "She's offering me a job as an internal investigator."

"Again?" Ben raises an eyebrow.

"I know. I'm starting to think someone's passing out my calling card."

"Or... rumors are spreading, and casinos want someone with your skills."

I roll my eyes, nudging him. "Come on. You know I'm staying put."

"And I'm glad," Ben says, his smile warming me.

I smile back, noticing how bright the day still is. Maybe that's why he asks, "What's on your mind, Rose?"

I turn my gaze to the horizon, where red and orange spill into the sea as the sun prepares to set. "Just feeling grateful—to have you, and everyone else—through all the ups and downs on our cruises."

Ben pulls me closer, his hand rubbing my arm gently. "We're the lucky ones. You're one of a kind, Rose. I wouldn't want to be solving murders or sailing these seas with anyone else."

I laugh, heart melting in the warmth. "Maybe we stick to cruising without the murders for a while."

I really hope so.

But if there's one thing I've learned, it's that those things aren't always up to us. Call it luck or fate—a quiet cruise or a murder onboard—either way, if luck or fate aren't on our side, we'll still make it work... like we always have.

Unlock the FREE Prequel:
Visit – https://BookHip.com/XJPXXHQ
(Murder on the Midnight Tide)

The saga starts with **_"Murder on the Midnight Tide,"_** where secrets simmer beneath the surface and danger lurks in the shadows.

Click below to immerse yourself in a world of suspense and mystery, where the only way out is to uncover the truth before it's too late: **_"Murder on the Midnight Tide,"_**

Get ready for the heart-pounding adventure as the voyage begins.

Sneak Peek

A deadly murder, a missing artifact, and Rose with Rex in a race to catch a killer.

Rose Dela Cruz thought she was finally getting a break. A few days aboard the Midnight Tide to escape the chaos of her private investigation business. But when a rude guest is found dead, her peaceful getaway quickly spirals into a nightmare.

Security insists it's a simple accident, but Rose knows better. She saw something—just a glimpse—but it's enough to make her heart race. The more she digs, the more she realizes everyone on board is hiding something. With her loyal Beagle, Rex, and her sister Stacy at her side, Rose begins to unravel a tangled web of lies, hidden motives, and a chilling riddle that only deepens the mystery.

As the clues start to fall into place, the danger escalates. Rose is racing against time to expose the killer before the Midnight Tide reaches its final destination—because if she doesn't, she might not survive to see another sunrise.

Unlock the FREE Prequel:
*Visit – https://BookHip.com/XJPXXHQ
(Murder on the Midnight Tide)*

Chapter 1

"I don't think this is a lead, Mrs. Reed."

I bite back my frustration as my contact rambles on, her voice fading into the background like a distant hum. My gaze drifts to the window, where the sun casts a warm glow over the Phoenix skyline, the iconic South Mountain rising proudly in the distance. The mix of desert and city stretches endlessly below me, traffic flowing like a restless river—each car a tiny vessel lost in the rush-hour chaos. I can't help but wonder, more than I'd like to admit, if those rocks down there might finally put an end to my relentless headache. And would the lizards appreciate the meal?

"Yes, I know about Jason Fink's new business," I reply, my old laptop humming in agreement, a tired six-year-old machine that could use a break as much as I can. "Seeing him with someone outside of work isn't a scoop. Honestly, I don't care who he's with. He's an adult, Mrs. Reed. He can do as he pleases."

I pinch the bridge of my nose, the pressure doing little to ease my rising irritation. "Mrs. Reed, I think there's a misunderstanding here. I'm a private investigator, not a gossip columnist. Do you have an actual case to report about Jason Fink?" "Goodness, no!" she exclaims, her tone scandalized. "He's a family friend. I have nothing against him at all."

My fingers tighten, as if I can crush the headache into submission. "Okay, then. Is there anything of interest you'd like to share with me?" A long pause stretches between us before she finally responds. "Well, I did see a man rescue a family from a car accident this morning." My heart skips a beat. Why on earth didn't she lead with this? I shove my frustration aside and focus on the potential lead. "You did? Perfect! Where? What happened?" I scramble to open a new Word document, eager to jot down every detail.

"Oh, it's a marvelous story! The handsome young police officer, you see, and he—" I end the call, my patience finally spent. Slowly, I close my laptop, resting my hands on either side, staring at the chipped edge of my desk. I contemplate bashing my head against it for good measure, but hesitate, glancing at the family portrait beside my computer. Ama and Ina smile at me from our last family reunion in the Philippines, their warmth anchoring me.

It's been three weeks since my last client. Not the longest dry spell I've faced, but maddening nonetheless. Cruz Secure Solutions—a clever pun on our surname, courtesy of my sister—remains a fledgling business, which means enduring these dry stretches. What I don't expect are the dozens of prank calls, desperate husbands badmouthing me to their elite friends, or the dirty looks I receive as I walk through my own hometown of Phoenix.

Stacy often reminds me I should've anticipated the backlash. She has a lot of opinions about what I should do. Speaking of her, a knock interrupts my thoughts. I sweep my bangs off my forehead, irritation flaring but curiosity piquing. "The office is closed for lunch!" I call out, my voice reverberating in the small space. "Come back later, please!"

The knocking continues, persistent. "The office is closed," I repeat, annoyance creeping in, but the door swings open before I can stand. "You're hilarious if you think lunch is going to keep me away, Rose," Stacy teases, leaning against the doorframe, a paper bag in hand and a mischievous grin lighting up her face.

She usually dresses impeccably for her logistics job, exuding that charming professional demeanor. But beneath the polished exterior, she's a whirlwind of laughter and excitement, quick with a witty remark. People often say I'm the steak knife to her butter. If we weren't so different, we could easily pass for identical twins with our straight black hair and blunt bangs. Mine end at my ears, and thankfully, my shorter stature and more casual style keep us distinct.

Stacy strolls over to my desk, her eyes sparkling with mischief. She mentioned her visit last week, and I knew it meant my work would take a backseat. She sets the bag down next to my laptop and plants a quick kiss on my forehead. "I brought you some adobo!" she announces, pulling up a stool and plopping down beside me.

"You're a lifesaver," I reply, eagerly clearing space to dig into the food. The fragrant aroma of the classic Filipino marinade wraps around me like a warm hug, easing the tension in my shoulders. "Today—no, this month has been a train wreck," I mutter.

"Capital T, capital R?" she smirks. "Even capital I-N." Stacy gasps in mock horror. "Not the I-N!"

I snort and elbow her playfully, grateful for a moment of levity. While I eat, she leans over, grabbing a few documents from my filing cabinet. Her brow furrows as she reads through them. "Is this..." She waves a paper at me. "Is this all your reports for the month?"

I nod. The "pile" consists of only two or three sheets at most, and fatigue is starting to show. Stacy whistles, placing a hand on my shoulder. "Wow, you weren't kidding. At least you got a little break...?" I shake my head. "You'd think so, but no. For every case I can take, I get ten phone calls from people who have no clue what a private investigator does."

Stacy sets the papers down, her expression shifting to something playful. "So... what you're saying is that you need a vacation?" I raise an eyebrow. "What I'm saying is that I need better work." She holds up her hands defensively. "Right, right! What I'm hearing is that you need a vacation, right?"

"Stacy." She rummages through her purse, pulling out two coupons, waving them enticingly. "Before I flew in, there was a company party for the CFO's birthday," her grin grows wider. "I won a top slot in the raffle!" I toss my empty lunch container into the trash and turn to face her, reluctance clear. "So, you're saying you didn't just fly down to visit because you love me and I'm your sister? You came to drag me into a vacation?"

"It's a cruise ship in Scotland!" she beams, her excitement palpable. "A month-long trip—total relaxation, all expenses paid except the flight." "I can't afford a flight," I protest. She waves her debit card enticingly, her determination unwavering. I let out a long, weary sigh. "Stacy, I really don't know…"

"I know you don't. But I do. You're a workaholic with no work, and this is a guilt-free way to relax." She gestures at my office, cluttered with crumpled notes and case files. "Don't even try to convince me you've accomplished anything productive cooped up in here. When you're not working, you're just stressing about work. Get one of your coworkers to take over the phone, and come with me."

I massage my temples, knowing she's right even if I don't want to admit it. She wraps an arm around my shoulders, and I look into her doe-like eyes. "We can have the best sister vacation ever." She jostles me playfully. "With drinks, parties, and handsome men to flirt with—just the ultimate sister bonding experience! Please, Rose? For me?"

I release a deep, resigned sigh, reaching up to ruffle her hair. "Fine, Stacy," I say, glancing at the ticket again. "I'll go. For you."

Chapter 2

The Midnight Tide looms before me, a majestic ship sparkling against the backdrop of a clear blue sky. It's pristine and grand, filled with people far wealthier than I could ever imagine being. The sight is slightly off-putting, especially after the relaxing flight from Phoenix to the Port of Ayr. Stacy, as always, spoils me—despite my protests—by booking us first-class seats. Yet, even against my better judgment, the beauty of the Scottish countryside captivates me. The port, with its blend of industrial charm and upscale travelers, possesses a unique allure.

I stick close to Stacy as we grab our luggage, weaving through the throngs of elegantly dressed passengers. Her arm loops through mine as if she expects me to bolt at any moment, which honestly isn't entirely out of the question. "This place is stunning," she breathes, her eyes sparkling as we finally reach the back of the line. "I missed Scotland so much! Remember last year's conference in London? They sent us to Edinburgh, and it was breathtaking. It feels so good to be back, doesn't it?" She glances at me, and I shoot her a skeptical look. "Sure, Stacy. Whatever you say."

"Oh, come on! You can't tell me you're not excited to see this!" She gestures animatedly toward the bright white-and-red ship, her enthusiasm infectious. I can't deny there's a flicker of anticipation in my chest, but it's tempered by anxiety. "There are a lot of important-looking people here," I murmur, scanning the crowd. As if on cue, I catch the dismissive gazes of at least three individuals who look me up and down, their expressions dripping with judgment.

Stacy narrows her eyes, clutching me tighter and glaring daggers until they finally look away. "Don't pay them any mind," she whispers. "You're here with me, and that means you're representing Ambrosia Industries." "Are people actually going to believe that?" Anxiety twists in my stomach as I glance down at my outfit. It's nice, sure, but nowhere near the designer labels flaunted by the other guests.

"Not everyone here is from Ambrosia. They're not going to kick you off the ship just because they think you're an imposter." Stacy hugs me briefly and steps forward in line, her sympathy palpable. "Your ticket is valid. If anyone gives you trouble, they'll have to deal with me. Don't worry, okay? I'll make sure you have the best time possible." I twist my mouth in reluctance, not wanting to argue. Instead, I tug my rolling suitcase behind me and follow her. "If you say so. Just tell me where I can and can't go. I don't want to wander into some high-society smoking room and have to scoot out like I've crashed a party I wasn't invited to."

Just as I finish my thought, I collide with something solid and stumble back, caught off guard. A man in line hasn't moved with the rest of us, and while Stacy deftly avoids him, I crash directly into his back. He turns around, glaring at me through tiny yet furious eyes, clearly unamused by the encounter. "Watch where you're going," he snaps, his voice gruff. I take a step back to regain my balance before I can even respond.

He's older, with beady eyes framed by scraggly white hair and a nose that looks like it's seen better days. His hat and coat are clean but clearly well-worn, and flanking him are two other men, their faces etched with surprise at his outburst. "Can't you people pay attention for once?" he barks.

The aggression startles me, but I quickly shake off my surprise. "Excuse me? You're the one who didn't move with the line," I shoot back, annoyance bubbling to the surface. "I would have if you hadn't tried to run me down," he retorts, crossing his arms. "I was walking toward the line. It was an accident! And you're still blocking it," I point out, my voice rising slightly.

"I don't want to hear your backtalk, ma'am. Who even are you?" He waves his hand dismissively at me. His companions exchange nervous glances, and before they can intervene, the old man continues his tirade. "The crew should have boarded the ship before the guests, and I'm certain they wouldn't want you dressed like that."

Heat rushes to my cheeks, but instead of feeling embarrassed, anger ignites within me. Before I can respond, Stacy steps protectively in front of me, her demeanor fierce. "I'm sorry, but I don't know who you think you are. I'd suggest you stop insulting my sister," she says, her eyes narrowing dangerously. "She's not just with my company; she's my sister. And I'll be frank with you—how I handle my family is very different from how I deal with my work."

The old man splutters, his broken nose scrunching in disbelief. "Well, your sister should act like she belongs here," he mutters, his tone condescending. Before I can retort, one of his companions places a hand on the old man's shoulder, cutting him off. "I apologize for my colleague's attitude," the older man says, stepping forward with a sheepish grin. His partner, who looks strikingly similar, follows closely behind. "He can come off as a bit... brash sometimes."

Stacy stands her ground, arms crossed like a fierce bodyguard. "That's one way to put it." "Don't patronize me, Thomas," the old man snaps, shaking off the hand on his shoulder. "Robert, please don't cause a scene. We're not even on the boat yet." The other man's tone suggests he's used to managing this behavior.

The old man huffs and turns away from us. As he does, Stacy starts again. "I expect an apology to my sister before the end of the—"

"No, Stacy—" I cut her off, my voice rising as I step back into view, flashing a quick smile at the ginger-haired man who's been watching us. "It's okay. I had a feeling something like this would happen."

"Still, that doesn't make it right," Stacy insists. The man frowns sympathetically and, to my surprise, extends his hand. "My name is Toby Gibson. Dr. Robert Franz over there and I are leading an excavation of some Celtic ruins along the shores of North Scotland. If he gives you any more trouble, please come to me, and I'll set him straight." As he speaks, he nods toward the old man, who shuffles further along in line.

I take his hand, hesitant, but his smile is warm enough to ease my tension. "I appreciate that, Mr. Gibson. I'm Rose Dela Cruz, and this is my sister, Stacy." I gesture toward her, and her expression softens, slipping back into her professional demeanor. "I'm a liaison for Ambrosia Industries. We're here on vacation to enjoy the sights. I've heard of your excavation, Mr. Gibson. Are you working with your brother?"

Toby's smile widens as he gestures to the man beside him. "Yes, I am! This is Darren, my co-foreman." "Pleasure to meet you both!" I reply, genuinely pleased. Darren, younger with his hair tied back in a ponytail, offers a shy smile that is less wide but equally sincere. "We're really sorry for Dr. Franz's behavior. Is there anything we can do to make it up to you two ladies?"

I open my mouth to decline, but of course, Stacy cuts me off. "Well, I don't think we'd say no to an escort on the ship." She shoots Darren a flirty smile, her confidence radiating. "You two can talk about your excavation; I've always had a keen interest in Celtic history." Stacy quickly moves ahead, and the two men follow, exchanging glances of intrigue when they think she isn't looking.

I try not to roll my eyes as I grab my luggage and carefully navigate the throngs of wealthy guests, avoiding any further collisions. As Stacy engages the two archaeologists, I find myself awestruck by the grandeur of the ship.

Unlock the FREE Prequel:
Visit – https://BookHip.com/XJPXXHQ
(Murder on the Midnight Tide)

Printed in Dunstable, United Kingdom